Lily
and the Shining Dragons

Lily reached out, and wrapped both hands around the strange soft stone of the dragon's body. Scales itched and glinted against her fingers, even though she couldn't see them, and the carving glowed brighter still. She could feel magic thrumming eagerly through the stone, like a warm little heart beating. And the eagerness! Something so wanted to break free.

But it couldn't, quite.

Lily's head swam, and Henrietta snarled. 'Lily, stop!'

Half-fainting, Lily's hands slid away from the stone, and she shook herself wearily.

Almost, something whispered gratefully. Soon!

Lily
and the Shining Dragons

HOLLY WEBB

ORCHARD

ORCHARD BOOKS
338 Euston Road, London NW1 3BH
Orchard Books Australia
Level 17/207 Kent Street, Sydney, NSW 2000

First published in the UK in 2012 by Orchard Books

ISBN 978 1 40831 350 3

Text © Holly Webb 2012

A CIP catalogue record for this book is available from the British Library.

3 5 7 9 10 8 6 4

Printed in Great Britain

Orchard Books is a division of Hachette Children's Books,
an Hachette UK company.

www.hachette.co.uk

For Alice, who told me to hurry up and finish it

ONE

'Is it not a real saw?' Lily asked doubtfully, staring at it as Daniel held it up. It looked real. Cleaner and shinier than most of the stagehands' tools, but just as sharp. It glinted wickedly.

'Oh, no, it's quite real,' Daniel assured her sunnily. 'It has to be: Georgie will walk amongst the audience carrying it, so they can check.'

'Then how...?' Lily stared at him worriedly. 'You're not asking me to do a spell, are you?' she asked, her voice edged with suspicion.

'Are you mad?' Daniel raised his eyebrows. 'After the Queen's Men turning up to investigate us last week? We nearly got arrested for forbidden magic, Lily; I'm not that stupid. We're on dangerous ground as it is. No, this is

…usion. In other words, completely
…d, exchanging a proud look with Sam,
…agehand who had constructed the Vanishing
…et that made their act famous. 'It's genius, it really
…. This Saturday night, that's when we'll unveil it. Always
a good audience on Saturdays.' Then he sighed, stroking
a hand lovingly over the polished wood contraption in
front of them. 'But it's only going to work with someone
as small as you, Lily.' He eyed her sister, Georgie,
measuring her up. 'You might just fit in, but you're
a good bit taller than she is. And all the girls in the ballet
troupe are too big; there's no chance they'll be able to do
it, even though they keep asking me if I don't want
a more experienced assistant, now that we're all popular.
No, I'm going to have to look for someone your age.'

Lily sniffed. 'And then not feed her, I suppose.'

Daniel nodded. 'Or not much, certainly,' he said,
quite seriously. 'It would be most unfortunate if she were
to stick.' Then he blinked. 'Oh. You were joking.'

'You haven't found anyone suitable yet?' Lily asked
anxiously. 'We need to leave soon. Next week, I thought.
As soon as you find girls to replace us. There was no one
at the theatrical agency?'

'They were useless,' Daniel said with disgust.
'I interviewed five girls, and without exception, when
I showed them the cabinets, all they did was giggle, and

say that they couldn't possibly.' He frowned at her worriedly. 'I wish you would stay. Both of you. And not just for the sake of the act. Or if you must go, I still don't see why you can't fly to the continent. I hate the idea of you somewhere in England by yourselves, when you could be discovered and arrested at any moment.'

Lily sighed. 'We were on our own before, and no harm came to us.'

Sam snorted, and Daniel threw up his hand crossly. 'Because you ended up here! You just happened to hit on a theatre, somewhere half of us hate the Queen's Men even more than you magicians do.' He stared at them anxiously. 'Tell me I can stop searching for new girls for the act. Just stay with us, where you're safe.'

'But we aren't!' Georgie shivered. 'Mama's already sent Marten after us. It'll be Mama herself chasing us next, I know it.'

'We can't stay in one place much longer,' Lily agreed. 'And we need to be able to fight back against Mama.' She swallowed. 'When she does find us.' She was almost certain that Mama would, one day soon. 'Staying here doesn't help us lift the spells Mama put on Georgie, Daniel.' She shivered. 'Now I've seen Queen Sophia, Mama's plan seems even worse. I half understand her – I mean, I hate what the queen has done. It isn't just that she's imprisoned our father, she's made me and Georgie and all the other magician children into something we're not. She's stopped us being ourselves, we've had to deny what's most special about us, because of the Decree. But I don't want to kill her. Mama means to use Georgie to kill the queen, Daniel. She wants the magic back. Magicians back in power, the way it was centuries ago, when our kind were flying around on dragons and all as rich as anything. She's not going to stay quietly shut away at Merrythought House any longer. Mama's mad, I think,' she added in a small voice. 'It's driven her that way, being penned up on the island all this time. She really does mean to kill the queen, and somehow those spells are going to make Georgie do it for her. She won't give up on her without a fight.'

'Or you,' a small, gruff voice added. 'She has her plans for you now too, remember.'

Until they'd escaped, Lily and Georgie had lived shut away from the rest of the world, with only their mother and a few very well-paid servants. The girls had fled Merrythought after they realised that their mother had kept Georgie under a spell for years, while she trained her in strange magics, which they still didn't understand. The dark spells Georgie had been learning were all still locked inside her, but they hadn't been working as well as Mama wanted. She had been getting angrier and angrier with Georgie, who'd grown sadder, and quieter, as the spells stole her spirit away.

Then the girls had overheard their mother saying to Marten, her maid, that she had no use for Georgie any more. She was planning to get rid of her – as she had the others. The two sisters hadn't known what this meant, but then they'd found a photograph album, with a sad little collection of pictures of their two older sisters – who never grew older than Georgie. Their magic had failed to satisfy Mama too. Georgie and Lily had no choice but to run away.

Lily picked Henrietta up, and held her close. There was something comforting about the black pug dog's sleek fur, and the certain ticking of her heart, even when she was saying the most uncomforting things. Even the existence of Henrietta made Lily feel happier – she had created the dog herself, or summoned her, she wasn't really sure which, from the portrait of her Great-Aunt Arabel that stood in the passage at home. It looked decidedly unbalanced now, without the small black dog Arabel had been holding. Arabel's expression had changed too. It strongly suggested that if she could get out of the painting, and get her hands on her great-niece, she would be wringing her neck.

'I know...' she murmured. 'I bet she'd rather use Georgie if she can, though. With me she'd have to start all over again.'

Henrietta sniffed. 'She wants you because Georgie isn't good enough.'

Georgie coughed. 'I am here, in case you'd forgotten,' she said sweetly. She didn't always get on with Henrietta, who thought she was feeble. Unfortunately, sometimes Lily had to agree. She adored Georgie, but her big sister had a definite feeble streak.

'I hadn't.' Henrietta waited, staring at her, in case Georgie was planning to deny it, but Georgie only went pink and looked miserable.

'The spells might not have worked when we were back at Merrythought, and Mama was teaching you them, but they work now! That's the problem!' Lily pointed out. 'They work too well. That wolf-thing you made was so good it nearly ate you, as well as tearing Marten to bits.'

'And me.' Henrietta nodded.

Lily had always hated Marten, her mother's maid, without really knowing why. It had been horribly unsurprising to learn that the black-clad creature wasn't human. Marten had been a construct of thousands upon thousands of intricately layered spells. Her mother's work of art.

The work of art had followed them to London, like some sort of magical bloodhound. Marten had been sniffing for traces of the spells that the girls' mother had woven into Georgie. She had been sent to drag them back. Mama had been on the point of giving up on Georgie, but the magic was starting to work in her now, seeping out whenever Georgie gave it a chance. Which wasn't often. Georgie had locked her own magic away deep inside, frightened of what she might let out with it.

It was Mama's own fault she had lost Marten, Lily thought, smiling to herself. It was almost funny now, a few days afterwards. But at the time, when she'd had to stand and watch her sister being dragged away, with Marten's blackish claws stabbing into her throat, it had not been funny at all. Then Georgie's terror had let the spells come slinking out, and it was Mama's own magic that had destroyed her servant. A huge wolf, made from London dust, and a trickle of blood from Georgie's scratched neck. The grey-red beast had turned on Marten, tearing away lumps of greenish spell-flesh, until she was only a pile of black clothes, and rustling dust.

Henrietta, however, had been rather put out by the wolf, as it was basically a much larger dog than she was, which offended her pride. 'The spells are there, inside her, no question. But she doesn't know what she's doing with them! Do you?' she added to Georgie, with a little snap at the hem of her skirt.

'Don't you dare bite that! This dress is new!' Georgie hissed back. She wasn't at all feeble about her clothes.

Being at the theatre, and let loose in the costume wardrobe, she had discovered that she infinitely preferred sewing to spells. 'I can't help not being to control the magic. It was made that way, wasn't it? I'm not supposed to be able to control it. Mama has the key, somehow…' Her voice trailed away. 'Ugh, how horrid. Like a sort of wind-up doll…'

'But if we find our father,' Lily explained to Daniel, 'there's a chance that he will have the – the key, too. Or at least, he'll be able to help us work it out.' She sighed. 'Well, he's the only other magician we know about, apart from Mama. He'll have to help. And we have to find him.' She sighed.

'If he isn't part of the plot as well,' Henrietta muttered.

Lily glared at the dog disapprovingly. She was trying to cheer Georgie up, not make her worse.

'He isn't. I'm sure he isn't. The letter, remember? He said he wasn't!' But Georgie was wringing her hands together worriedly. She wasn't sure at all, and neither was Lily. Their father was their only hope – but it was a slim one.

'How are you going to find your dad?' Sam asked slowly, and the girls looked up in surprise. They had almost forgotten he was there. Sam was never talkative, but he had been one of the first people in the theatre, apart from Daniel, to learn their secret, and they trusted him. Henrietta adored him, and he made a special fuss over her, saving her bits of his lunches. He had liked her even before he knew she could talk, and now he regarded her as a little wonder – much more exciting than the girls, even though Henrietta couldn't do magic herself.

Lily and Georgie looked at each other, and Georgie shrugged. 'He's in prison...'

'And the prison might be in London – that's where the letters to Mama came from. That's all we know. Really everything.' Lily sighed. Then she glanced at Daniel. 'Do all magicians end up in the same prison?' she asked him, frowning. 'I suppose it can't be just any old prison, can it? There must be special defences. Or guards who can stop spells. That's what Father's letter seemed to say. Although...that would probably mean they were using magic themselves, which is illegal, so I don't see how...' She swallowed, feeling suddenly a little sick. 'Unless they do something to the prisoners, to stop their magic working. Cut the magic out of them, or something horrible like that...'

Daniel hugged her. 'If they could do that, I think there would have been more fuss made about it. The old queen would have had it trumpeted from the rooftops.' He held Lily's shoulders, so he could look her in the eyes. 'They couldn't do it, Lily. There would have been problems from abroad, as well. It's only here that magic's illegal, remember. Magicians are flourishing in most of the rest of the world. Even here, if they renounce their magic, the way your mother swore to the Queen's Men she had done, magicians are free. Under suspicion, always, and watched, but free. Your father must have refused to give his magic up.'

Lily smiled. She could understand that. She couldn't imagine living without hers, even though Georgie seemed not to mind. She loved the permanent sense of tingly, sparkling possibility inside her. The way it rushed into her fingers so eagerly as soon as she called it. Even the cross, jumpy feeling under her skin when she'd cooped it up for too long, and it was aching to be set free. And she could put up with spells always making her hair curlier, although she would have loved sleek, straight hair like Georgie's.

She felt closer to her father than she ever had, realising that he must have been the same way. He had curly hair too, she remembered, thinking of the wedding portrait in her mother's green leather photograph album. He had been in prison for most of her life, and she had no memories of him.

'Can you visit prisons?' Lily asked Sam, rather doubtfully.

Sam snorted with laughter. 'If you pay the guards.

Or if you're bringing in missionary tracts. But like you say, Miss Lily, it might all be different in a magicians' prison.'

Daniel was scowling, running his fingers through his black hair, so it stood up on end even more than usual. 'I must say, it would be a weight off my mind if you were to find him. You're too young to be without anyone, the way you are.'

Lily smiled. Daniel sounded like a respectable old man with side-whiskers. Not the seventeen-year-old owner of a scandalous theatre.

'Magicians' prison. All I know about it is that it's a secret. Closely guarded – no one knows where it is. The kind of thing you can be imprisoned for even asking about. Although you'd think there would be something about it in one of my books,' Daniel murmured now. Books on magic were outlawed just as magic itself was, but Daniel had done a great deal of research for his conjuring act, and owned several banned volumes. He wandered towards the steps at the front of the stage, muttering to himself, and making for his office by the grand entrance to the theatre.

'If you want this trick ready in two days' time,' Sam called after him, 'don't you think we ought to see if she fits? I know Miss Lily won't be the one doing it for long, but you did tell that journalist that was here yesterday that there was to be a new trick, remember? The Devil's Cabinet is old hat now, you said. Vandinovksi at the Ottoman Palace has the trick almost as well as we do. This weekend, you said. Come to the show on Saturday, you said.'

Daniel turned round, red-faced. 'Yes. I quite forgot.' He sighed. 'And to be honest, Lily, I don't think I'll be able to find out what you need in any of my books. I'd have remembered, I'm sure. I've read them all so many times.' He pushed up his shirtsleeves in a businesslike sort of way. 'So. Here we are.'

Lily looked at the wooden cabinet in front of them, and nibbled her top lip doubtfully. She still didn't see how it was going to work. Admittedly, she never could see through Daniel and Sam's contraptions before they were explained to her, but then they'd never involved very sharp saws, till now. She was particularly anxious to make sure this one worked. She did wish Daniel wasn't quite so butterfly-minded. When one was going to be sawn in half, one liked to know that the person with the saw was really paying attention.

'Now, there is a very, very slight risk with this trick,' Daniel explained, as he undid the shiny brass catches on the cabinet.

'Of being cut in half?' Lily asked, taking a step backwards.

'No! Of course not. Just – well, it's possible we might catch your toes. If you're not quick enough.' Daniel smiled at her winningly. 'We'd only nick them…' he said, in an earnest sort of voice.

'She isn't doing it!' Georgie and Henrietta both snapped, at practically the same time. Then they glared at each other.

'How would you cut my toes, when you're sawing through the middle of me?' Lily peered at the cabinet. Daniel had undone it now, so that it looked like a table, with two hinged boxes that folded down over it. The table had chains, and looked most unpleasant.

'I'll show you. Look, lie down here.' Lily stared at the table suspiciously, and Daniel sighed. 'I won't even pick up the saw. I promise. Here, Henrietta, sit on it.' He laid it on the floor, and the black pug planted her paws firmly on the handle.

'Go on. I want to see,' she commanded. 'Hurry up, Lily.'

'You lie down here – smiling, and waving, you know, so that the audience sees you aren't afraid.' Daniel ignored Henrietta snorting here. 'And we put the chains around your arms, and your feet. The feet are very important.'

'I know!' Lily hissed. 'Which is why I'd like to keep my toes!'

Daniel exchanged a look with Sam, a rolled eyes sort of look, but Lily didn't care. 'Lily, I haven't even got the saw – let me just explain how it works!'

Lily wriggled gingerly into the box, and allowed Daniel to drape the chains over her. 'Of course, for the show, we'll make a fuss with padlocks, that sort of thing,' he explained. 'And then I fold the boxes down over you – and now you see, your feet are hidden, yes? But the audience can still see your face. I think it would be good if you looked just a little nervous now.'

Henrietta snickered, and Lily wriggled uncomfortably. The box fitted tightly around her neck, and it felt very strange having just her head sticking out at the end.

'Not quite that nervous, please.' Daniel frowned at her. 'Now, do you see the tiny gap between the two boxes?'

'No!' Lily snapped. 'I can't see anything down here.'

'Ah, no, of course not. Well, there is one, and that's where the saw goes, you see.'

'But then where does Lily go?' Georgie asked worriedly. 'I can see just a scrap of her dress through the gap – you can't saw through there!'

'She slips her feet out of the chains – because that hasp that fitted over them looks tight, but actually there's plenty of room, Lily, especially if you lift your ankles a little bit. You pull your feet out, and curl up in this end of the box. It's really very simple. The way the box is made, it looks shallower than it really is, that's all. And the audience knows that you're chained down, so they'll be convinced that I've cut you in half! Isn't it wonderful?'

'I suppose so…' Lily admitted. She had a feeling the illusion would look better when viewed standing up, rather than from inside.

'What about the toes?' Henrietta demanded, getting up, and standing on her hind legs to sniff at the gap between the boxes.

'Ah. Yes. Lily, try to slip your feet out, and curl up, the way I described.'

Lily wriggled her ankles experimentally, and found that it was just as Daniel said, there was plenty of room. She drew her knees up to her chest, hugging her feet in as tightly as she could.

'You've done it?' Daniel asked hopefully, and Lily nodded. She was squashed so closely into the first box that she could hardly breathe, let alone talk.

'Good! Now, you see, in the performance Georgie and I will work the saw back and forth – with a suitable effort, you know, as though we were really cutting through you – and then these steel plates slot in, here and here. And again, I'll force them down, as though there's resistance—'

'Ugh…' Lily muttered. Daniel's eyes were shining with excitement; it was rather sickening.

'So then the box hinges apart, like so!' Daniel flipped the catches, and dramatically swung the table so it split in two. It was rather an anticlimax to see Lily's black button boots, squashed up into her petticoats – Sam even averted his eyes. 'Well, of course the audience will only see the steel plates. You fit perfectly, Lily. But you mustn't stick your feet out any further…'

'But how will I know if they're far enough in?' Lily asked him, wriggling anxiously. 'And more to the point, how will *you* know?'

'I won't, that's the slight drawback with this apparatus. But it will be fine! You've got lots of room. Really!'

'Are you worrying about the new trick?' Henrietta asked. She was lying on the bed next to Lily, on her back, with her little black paws waving in the air. It was an undignified position, which she never would have taken up in company.

Lily stared down at her fondly. It was mid-afternoon, and she'd been planning to sleep, as the variety show ran on late, and the second part of their act was the finale. But she'd given after up after a few minutes' irritable wriggling, and now had her chin on her hands. She was vaguely reading one of the illustrated papers that someone had left lying in the theatre. 'No. Well, maybe a little. I don't like the sound of those steel plates. And I wish Daniel didn't sound so gory about it all.'

Henrietta leaned sideways, and licked one of Lily's hands. 'Mmm. He was enjoying all that talk of saws. Silly little boy.'

'Exactly.' Lily sighed. 'But that wasn't actually what I was worrying about. I was thinking about Father.'

'Hmf.' Henrietta twisted athletically, and turned herself the right way up, staring at Lily with round, intelligent eyes. 'Where to find him?'

Lily nodded. 'We haven't a clue, have we? Not even the slightest. It's all very well telling Daniel we're leaving next week, but where shall we *go*?'

'Mmmm.' Henrietta laid her chin on her paws, staring thoughtfully at the grubby brick of the wall. The girls slept at the theatre, as part of their arrangement with Daniel, and the room was not luxurious. But it was safe, and that was all that mattered. Or it had been safe…

'Where is your sister?' Henrietta demanded, looking up suddenly.

'Guess!'

'In that tatty seamstresses' parlour, *again*?' Henrietta demanded irritably.

'She likes it.' Lily shrugged, her voice tinged with

a little disbelief. Neither of the girls had ever been taught to sew – it wasn't something that Mama had cared about in the slightest – but Georgie had discovered something she was good at, at last. Maria, the wardrobe mistress, had taken her on as a sort of unofficial apprentice.

'She should be working on her magic. Or at least helping you to plan what we do next. If she wants to break your mother's hold over her, she needs to put some effort in!'

Lily nodded. 'I know. But I think she's even more frightened of leaving the theatre than I am. You know she hardly ever goes out. And the last time she did, Marten attacked her.'

'If your sister is too afraid to use her magic, she's not going to be much help finding your father's prison, either.' Henrietta grunted with irritation. 'It's up to us. As usual.'

'I wonder if we could do something like Marten's hunting?' Lily mused. 'Do you think you could sniff out the prison? It would be a whole clutch of magicians, that might make it easier.'

Henrietta's pug wrinkles deepened. 'Well, I could if they were doing magic, but they aren't, are they? That's the point. Your father said in that letter we found that they were suppressing his magic, somehow.'

Lily sighed, and rolled on to her back, her arm

around Henrietta, staring up at the dirty ceiling. The damp patches seemed to move and grow darker through her tired eyes, so that the dark castle-shaped blotch sprouted turrets, and unpleasant spikes here and there. It seemed very suitable, and Lily shivered.

'I suppose you can hardly follow a scent that's not even happening. It seemed such a good idea, just for a minute. Oh!' She sat up crossly, shaking the grey shapes out of her eyes. 'Someone must know where it is!'

'But we can't ask, can we?' Henrietta growled. 'Not without looking extremely suspicious. We need to find ourselves another magician. Someone who knows more about the world than we do. And doesn't mind risking being imprisoned, just for talking to us about it.' Then she growled again, staring at the door, and curled herself into a neat, doglike shape. Someone was coming.

Georgie flung the door open, and stood in the doorway. She looked happy, Lily thought, almost resentfully. It was clear she'd spent an enjoyable afternoon sewing with Maria, while Lily and Henrietta worried.

'Come on. It's time to dress.'

'Already?' Lily said wearily. Would-be rescuers had better keep earlier hours than theatre performers, she decided. Once they were no longer part of the act, she was going to sleep for a whole day. That would be before they were arrested, the gloomier side of her added. The Queen's Men were suspicious of Daniel and the girls already, even without Lily and Georgie sniffing around for magical prisons.

'I'll have to make you a new costume for the divided box trick,' Georgie said, looking Lily up and down critically in their cupboard-sized dressing room. 'Perhaps something eastern, with those floaty pantaloons. Otherwise it might be a bit undignified. I'll ask Maria.'

'Can't I just wear tights, like the ballet dancers?' Lily asked.

'No. Tights aren't proper.' Georgie shook her head sternly.

'I don't think being onstage at all is proper, Georgie.' Lily sniggered. 'Besides when have we ever cared about being proper? Our father's a criminal, you know, officially anyway.' She was silent a minute. 'And Mama *definitely* is one. Even if we're the only people who know.'

'All the more reason to keep up appearances,' Georgie muttered. 'We're supposed to be exiled princesses from the far north, remember. Princesses don't show their legs. If the Queen's Men come back, Lily, we have to look like…' Georgie paused. 'Like nice girls. Not the sort of people who ought to be arrested. Here. Let me fasten you up.'

Lily sighed. She had only just got used to the fussiness

of her blue costume, with its ribbons and flounces, and the complicated hook-and-eye fastening that was a nightmare to do up in a hurry. She didn't want another one. Still, it was pleasant to let Georgie hover over her, and prink her into shape. She didn't have to think, she could just sit, and be tweaked at.

'Ow!' Lily protested, as her sister raked a comb through her curls, and tried to pin them up. 'You know the pins won't stay in, why try?'

Georgie, whose own hair was now an intricate arrangement of swirls and sparkling paste jewels, shook her head. 'Oh, just shove the tiara on it then! Really, Lily, it's as if you're doing it on purpose.' She caught Lily's chin suddenly, and pulled her face round, so she could stare into her sister's eyes. 'Tell me you're not doing a spell to repel hairpins!'

Lily wriggled crossly. 'I don't like having my hair up! It's enough to have the tiara, isn't it? If you put it up the pins jab into me, and then they fall out in the middle of the act. It's distracting.' She looked up at Georgie, a little shamefaced. 'I didn't start it on purpose. But then...'

Georgie shook her head. 'You have so much magic, Lily. It scares me that you can use it for such little things.' She shivered. 'Be careful. If you keep a spell like that going all the time, who's to say you won't forget, and let someone see?'

'I won't. I promise.' She hugged Georgie tightly. 'I truly promise. Look, I've stopped it.' Lily ran a hand over her hair, as though she was wiping away a cobweb caught there. 'You can pin it up now. I'll make it stick.'

'But that's just as bad!' Georgie laughed, a little bitterly. 'I'm not really jealous, Lily. I know I could do it too, if I wasn't worrying about what might wake up inside me. But you just seem to use spells so easily. As if it's nothing.' She sat down on one of the rickety old chairs next to Lily, and stared at her little sister's messy, tangled curls. 'Oh, go on. There's the pins. You do it.' She shoved a box of pins and assorted shiny things along the table to Lily, and glared at her, her eyes wet.

'All right,' Lily whispered, miserably. 'You'd better watch the door.' Her sister was always holed up in the wardrobe, cocooned in sparkling fabrics. Safe. Lily had thought she was happy too. But she was wrong.

Looking apologetically up at Georgie, she poked her fingers into her curls, and twirled. Henrietta leaped on to her lap. She loved magic. Spells made her tail curl tighter, and now she watched bright-eyed as Lily's hair snaked itself into glossy brown locks, winding around themselves in delicate pleats and plaits. A shower of dull gold hairpins flew out of the box, and stabbed into the gleaming mass.

'Which jewels?' Lily asked humbly.

Georgie sighed. 'Those big diamondy ones. The bigger the better, for the stage, though they're vulgar as anything.'

Lily nodded, and the diamond clips appeared in her hair, sparkling merrily.

Georgie eyed her. 'Oh well. If you must risk us all being arrested, I suppose you might as well do it with nice hair.' Then she stalked to the dressing-room door. 'Come on then!' she snapped, but she was smiling, and Lily raced after her.

'Someone's watching you two.'

Lily looked up at Sam, panting a little. He'd caught her as she hurried offstage. They'd had three curtain calls, and she'd had to race back to the front of the stage and bow again and again before they could go, and let the trick cyclist troupe come on. The illusionist act seemed to be more popular every night.

'They're supposed to watch us, Sam. *Everyone's* supposed to be watching!'

'You know what I mean, missy. Don't be smart.'

Henrietta growled, very quietly, but she was eyeing Lily, not Sam. Lily stopped smiling, and shook her head. 'I won't. What do you mean? Who's watching?'

'A lady. Tall, looks like to me. Thin. *Very* thin, but not like it's natural. She's in one of the boxes, first tier, left of the stage.' He frowned. 'She's got a look of your sister, though I can't quite say how. That light hair, maybe.'

Lily went pale. 'Mama?' she faltered. But then Henrietta nipped her ankle crossly. 'Oh, no, not if she's thin. All right, I know it was stupid, Henrietta! But there's no one else…' She stopped. Actually, of course, she didn't know that. She and Georgie had always supposed they had no relatives, because Mama had never mentioned them.

'Want me to point her out?' Sam shuffled her towards the edge of the curtain.

Lily peered around it, careful not to sway the heavy velvet. The auditorium was packed, not a little crimson chair empty.

'There, see? With a boy next to her.' Sam nudged Lily, showing her a tall, regal-looking woman in one of the nearest boxes.

She had a good view there, Lily thought, the blood seeming to flow through her heart slower all of a sudden. A very good view. The gold-haired woman couldn't know that Lily was on the other side of the curtain. Lily would swear that she was hidden. But the woman was staring right at her.

Straight into Lily's eyes.

TWO

Lily ducked back into the wings, with Henrietta coiling anxiously around her ankles, and whimpering.

'Who is she?' Sam demanded. 'You look as though you're about to faint, Lily. What's happening? Is that your ma?'

Lily shook her head. 'I don't know who she is. But you're right, she does look like Georgie. A little. She was *looking* at me, Sam. She knows who I am.' She leaned against the wall, biting her lip. 'We have to go onstage again, at the end of the show. Our finale act. She'll be watching us again.'

'And I'll be watching her. I promise you. If I see anything that looks…nasty, I'll haul you offstage. All of you. Even if it means breaking the illusion. I won't let anyone hurt you.'

'You can't do that!' Lily sounded shocked. She and Georgie and Henrietta had only been theatre performers for a few weeks, but they had absorbed how important it was to keep the audience happy. The show must always go on.

'Watch me,' Sam muttered, leaning out to try and catch another glimpse of the skinny, gold-haired woman.

Lily smiled at him. She knew that she and Georgie would have to go onstage, and wave and smile and do everything the way they usually did it. And she knew that although Sam would do anything he could to help, if the woman in the stage-left box wanted to hurt Lily or Georgie somehow, he would be worse than useless. He would probably get himself hurt too, which was another thing for Lily to worry about.

Whoever she was, she'd used magic. Lily was sure. She'd *known* that Lily was behind the curtain peering out. Only magic could have told her that, and all magic was forbidden, by the Queen's Decree. The gold-haired woman was another magician in hiding. She had to be.

So even if Lily hadn't hated the idea of spoiling the show, she had to go back onstage. She had to show the gold-haired woman that she wasn't afraid, that she knew who had come to watch them. Lily would stare back, eye to eye. That way, the woman would want to meet them, surely? Then they would have what they needed. Another magician. Someone who might know where their father's prison was.

'Is she still there?' Lily hissed to Sam, as they waited in the wings to run on for the finale.

He nodded grimly, and Lily smiled.

'What are you two planning?' Daniel asked, looking at them suspiciously, and Georgie turned worried eyes on Lily.

'There's a magician in the left-hand box.' Lily lowered her voice and nodded towards it. 'A woman. Georgie, don't go into your dying duck act! We need a magician, don't you see? She might know where Father is. Just try and look…tempting.'

'Tempting!' Georgie hissed. 'I'm not a supper dish, Lily!'

'Not yet.' Sam exchanged a determined look with Daniel. 'I'll be watching them, don't you worry.'

'You can't.' Daniel shook his head. 'If she's a magician, we have to let Lily and Georgie protect everyone else. Lily, why didn't you say? We could have cleared the theatre. A fire. A typhus scare. Anything!'

'I didn't tell you because I knew that's what you

would say!' Lily snapped. 'Especially after Marten. I don't want to get away from her, I need to ask her things.' She shook out her glittery skirts, and assumed her stage smile, the one with lots of teeth. It did not go well with the determined scowl. 'So come on. Tempting, remember?'

And the curtains drew back.

'Nothing,' Lily snarled bitterly. 'Nothing, nothing, nothing! Not a word, or a note, or a message at the stage door. Nothing!'

Georgie nodded, and Lily could tell that she was trying not to look too relieved. They had got through the finale without too many mistakes – none, hopefully, that anyone but themselves had seen. Georgie's Northern Princess face had been more fixed than usual, perhaps, as she tried to stop staring at the stage-left box, but she had danced and twirled and been entranced just as usual. The new divided box act would have been a relief, Lily had thought, as she gathered up the artificial flowers that Daniel was strewing out of his sleeves. A welcome change, if only they were staying for it. The Devil's Cabinet and the levitation trick were growing stale.

She had been so sure. There was a magician come to see them. It was the next step – the clue they needed.

Daniel would have to find another pair of assistants even sooner than they had hoped.

But it had all come to nothing. The gold-haired woman had vanished out of the box between the curtain calls, and there had been no word from her since.

'I know she was staring at us,' Lily muttered. 'Why watch us like that, and then just disappear?'

Georgie shook her head, and simply went on rinsing out their silk stockings in a bowl of warm water. They only had one pair each, as they were hideously expensive, and she had to wash them between performances.

Suddenly Henrietta sat up on the bed, her tail flicking back and forth uncertainly. 'Listen! Something... There's a scent of magic. The proper stuff. For heaven's sake, girl, put that away!' she growled at Georgie. 'Smooth your hair.'

Georgie stuffed the bowl under the bed, and stood up looking guilty, and frightened.

Lily brushed down her skirt. There was no point trying to do anything to her hair without a spell, and right now, she didn't want to. It seemed – foolish. Better to keep everything under wraps, until they had some idea of what they were dealing with. She looked around the dingy room, and suddenly wished they'd made more fuss to Daniel about somewhere nicer to sleep. Or larger, so at least there was a place other than the bed to sit.

Then she shrugged, twisting her shoulders awkwardly. She'd never cared about the room before. It was a safe refuge from Mama and Marten. They had been *grateful*, and so they should have been. What had come over her?

'It can't be that magician.' Lily turned to Georgie, shaking her head uncertainly. 'They wouldn't have let her in the theatre. The front's still locked up this time of the afternoon, and the stagehands wouldn't let her just walk in the doors from the scene dock, would they?'

Georgie turned her head slowly, one side then the other. No.

But they knew it was her.

'She's coming,' Lily muttered, though there was no need for her to say.

The gold-haired woman was there, suddenly, in the doorway. The hair was coiled elegantly under a tiny black velvet hat, which matched the black velvet trimming on her dark red silk dress. It looked rather like one of the grandest costumes in the theatre wardrobe, only without the spangles, and the silk floss. It also looked expensive.

The dress had stopped Georgie being quite so frightened, Lily could tell. Her sister was eyeing the outfit hungrily, peering at the elegant way the overskirt was drawn up over the bustle at the back, and the velvet rosettes holding it in place. Her eyes were bright with admiration now, instead of fear.

But Lily was looking at the woman's face, and not her dress, and she was still scared. Henrietta was humming a low-toned growl, practically too quiet to hear. She had backed almost under the bed as the woman appeared in the doorway. Lily wished she could hide under the bed too.

The gold-haired woman smiled graciously around at all of them. With only a twitch at her skirt, she somehow managed to show that she thought the room was dirty, and they were unkempt, and she was demeaning herself even by letting her black lace petticoats trail over the dusty floor. It was impressive.

Lily stood on one foot, tucking the other behind her ankle, and trying to look as though she wasn't. The floor was so dirty, she didn't want to touch it any more than she absolutely had to. And her black cotton stocking had a hole...

'It doesn't...' she whispered to herself, shaking her head. And she put her foot down hard on the boards again. 'Or, anyway, Georgie darned it.'

The magician in the doorway smiled harder, showing teeth like pearls, and Lily's foot itched to curl itself away from the floor again. But she didn't. There was a squeaking of springs behind her, and she glanced round to see that Georgie was now sitting on their bed, with her knees drawn up to her chest. She was looking around the room as if it sickened her.

'Stop it!' Lily snapped, making the same snatching gesture she had used to pull the spell away from her hair. Henrietta raced forward, snapping at the woman's ruffled skirts, and dragging something almost invisible away in her teeth, the way she gathered up the strings of handkerchiefs, only this time she gulped, and wriggled, and coughed a little, and then stalked over to sit smugly at Lily's feet. Lily nodded at her, pleased. They hadn't known Henrietta could eat spells.

'My dear child, what?' The magician was still smiling, although her lips had thinned a little. 'I really don't know what you mean. And I do hope the dear dog is not fierce. I really cannot have a savage dog in my house.'

Lily could feel Henrietta pressed against her feet, growling. She wanted to talk, Lily could tell, but she wasn't sure if she ought to. Lily wasn't either. It was obvious now that the woman had been casting a spell on them as she walked down the corridor, one that made them feel dirty, and ashamed of their faded old room. But there was something strange about her. Lily had expected her to retaliate after they had torn away her spell, but she'd done nothing but smile. It was almost as if she hadn't noticed. And what was she talking about her house for?

'We seem to have missed out our introductions,' the woman purred sweetly. 'I am Lady Clara Fishe.' She looked at them expectantly, and Georgie wriggled off the bed, and bobbed a little curtsey. Ungraciously, Lily bent her knees very slightly. She could curtsey properly, of course, but she simply didn't want to. She wasn't used to people trying to put spells on her. Mama had hardly ever bothered even to see Lily, and Georgie had grown out of practising on her little sister years ago.

'Fishe with an e,' Lady Clara added, as though this made a great deal of difference.

Lily and Georgie only stared at her.

Lady Clara sighed, politely irritated by their stupidity. 'I am your *aunt*.'

Lily and Georgie exchanged a surprised glance, and then Georgie shook her head. 'We don't have an aunt. My lady.'

'Of course you do!' Lady Clara stared at them, her pale eyes bulging a little. She had a glamour on, Lily realised. Her eyes weren't as beautifully blue as they looked at first. The glamour had slipped, just a little, now that she was surprised. 'You are my sister Nerissa's children, aren't you?'

Lily swallowed, looking at the golden hair and pale eyes more closely. Mama. A taller, thinner, prettier Mama was glaring at them irritably. Lily's heart seemed to beat more slowly, as the blood went suddenly cold inside her. Why had they never known they had an aunt? Their mother's sister. What if Mama had sent her?

'I had thought you were older, but you look just like her. You, particularly.' She gestured at Georgie. 'Lucy? And – oh, what did they name the other one? Prudence?' She sniffed angrily. 'Such a ridiculous name! As if a child of Nerissa's would ever be prudent! After the way they behaved.'

She didn't know that their sisters were dead, Lily realised. That Mama had killed them, or so Lily and Georgie suspected. So she and Mama weren't close. The ice inside her melted a little, and she began to see more clearly.

She was suddenly quite a plain woman, Lily noticed, the glamour lost for a moment in her fury and disgust. Then it was as if a hand smoothed over her features, and they were sweetly regular again. But in that moment of forgetfulness, she had looked just like Mama. 'And clearly you aren't prudent at all. Showing off in some dreadful illusionist's act. With the cream of London society in attendance. Sooner or later, someone will notice the resemblance.' This time she kept hold of the glamour, but her pearly teeth were grinding.

'We aren't Lucy and Prudence,' Lily said slowly. There seemed no point in denying it. 'They're dead.'

Their aunt blinked. 'Indeed. How sad,' she added, not sounding sad in the least. 'Then you are?'

'Lily. And this is Georgiana.'

Lady Clara sniffed. 'Better than Prudence, I suppose. And where is my sister?' She glanced around the room, as though she expected them to be hiding their mother in a cupboard somewhere. 'Why on earth are you part of this – this disgusting charade? Has she finally run through all Peyton Powers' money, is that it?'

Lily felt Georgie's cold hand slip into hers, and she glanced up at her sister anxiously. Their aunt didn't seem to know about Mama's plot at all. She certainly didn't look like someone who wanted to assassinate the queen – but then, successful assassins probably didn't. 'Mama is still at Merrythought,' Lily admitted, clutching Georgie's hand tightly. 'We ran away.' Somehow, she didn't think their aunt would like them any less for admitting it. But it could still be a trap. Lily's fingers buzzed with stored-up magic. She was ready…

'You ran away. How very sensible…' Lady Clara put her head on one side, and eyed them thoughtfully. 'But the stage? Really?'

'We didn't intend to.' Lily shrugged. 'Mama was

trying to manipulate Georgie's magic. She was hurting her.' It was almost true. 'We had to get away. The theatre was accidental. But lucky,' she added stubbornly.

Lady Clara was turning pale, but she still had enough control of the glamour that she did it very prettily. She looked like a delicate china doll. 'Nerissa is still using magic then?' she whispered huskily. 'How can she be?'

Lily and Georgie exchanged a confused glance. They'd both felt the spell their aunt laid on them, that strange shame spell. And she definitely had a glamour on. 'She hides it from the Queen's Men, of course,' Lily explained hesitantly. 'But, Aunt,' – it felt very strange to call this unknown woman their aunt – 'you use magic.'

'I do not.' The colour rushed back into Aunt Clara's face. She was a cheap wooden doll now, with bright circles of red on her cheeks. 'Magic is wrong. It's dangerous. Dirty. Her dear Majesty was quite right to forbid it. I forswore magic as a young girl, as your mother and father should have done.'

'Maybe she doesn't know she's doing it?' Georgie breathed in Lily's ear. 'Do you believe her?'

Lily shrugged, a tiny little movement. She couldn't tell. Could their aunt's glamour be so closely woven into her now that she really didn't realise it was there? And the spell that had made them so ashamed of their room, and their clothes – she could imagine that might be one her aunt wove around herself unconsciously. Her beautiful, expensive dress, the gloves, the society manners – appearances were her life. She could be weaving the spell out of her own disgust, and projecting it on to everyone around her without even knowing it.

Still… Lily wasn't completely convinced. How had their aunt managed to get away with wafting around in a cloud of tiny spells for years? Unless she was actually very, very clever?

'Magic isn't dirty,' she muttered stubbornly.

Her aunt swayed gracefully across the room towards her. 'Oh but my dear, it is. Magic is wrong. Quite wrong. It has poisoned our bloodline, and we must cast it out.'

Lily swallowed the anger that was rising inside her, bringing a tide of magic with it. She longed to throw it at this stupid woman, and wrap it all round her, so that she could see how beautiful it was.

Henrietta pawed at her leg, and Lily picked her up. Aunt Clara smiled at the pug approvingly. 'I see it does have company manners after all.'

'And she is clearly mad,' Henrietta muttered, pretending to nuzzle Lily's cheek.

Lily nodded a little. 'Aunt, what did you mean before, about a savage dog in your house?'

Aunt Clara looked around the room, and for a moment her strange hidden magic flashed out again, and Lily saw their refuge as she did. Peeling wallpaper, grubby boards, the damp stains – but all magnified tenfold. She shivered, and her aunt nodded. 'You see? You can't possibly stay here. I may not have agreed with my sister.' She closed her eyes for a moment, and shuddered. 'I hope never to see her again, for that matter. But I cannot have my nieces frequenting a common theatre. Especially when the resemblance is so distinct.' She glanced at Georgie, and shuddered. 'We can only hope that once you are properly dressed, no one will recognise you in Marlborough Square.'

'You want us to live with you?' Georgie whispered doubtfully.

Aunt Clara nodded. 'I'm offering you a home. But you must promise to behave properly.' All of a sudden her society sweetness seemed to fall away, and she fixed them with a sharp, honest look. 'You know quite well what I mean. No magic. None at all.'

'We don't do magic now,' Lily told her, widening her eyes innocently. 'Our act is just that, Aunt. It's all an act. We could explain the illusions to you, but we're sworn to secrecy.'

Aunt Clara gave her a freezing glare. 'The sooner we get you out of here the better. I'm ashamed to find you so forward. Who knows what sort of degenerate manners you've learned in this place.'

'Lily, don't,' Georgie murmured in her ear, as Lily drew breath to answer back. 'We need her, remember? She's our magician. Our source. And she's family. She must have some idea where Papa is, surely.'

Lily let out an angry little sigh. Family didn't necessarily mean safe. Daniel and Sam and the others in the theatre had taken better care of her and Georgie than Mama ever had, even if the theatre wasn't respectable. She seethed, hating that she had to let their aunt say such things. But Georgie was right. They needed her.

'You won't send us back to our mother?' she asked, wrapping her arms more tightly around Henrietta. 'You won't tell her where we are, even?'

'I haven't seen or spoken to her in more than ten years.' Aunt Clara waved the idea away with a kid-gloved hand. 'Why would I tell her?'

'Why do you want us?' Lily frowned. She felt better now they weren't dancing around each other.

Her aunt smiled tightly, and brushed invisible dust from the folds of her skirt. 'I don't. But you can't stay here. It's very obvious to me that you're Nerissa's daughters, and sooner or later someone else will recognise you. I have spent years – a very many years – making everyone forget my unfortunate family connections. I have no intention of letting my two little nieces rake it all up again.'

'So you want us where you can see us?'

Aunt Clara's smile seemed to stretch around her teeth. 'Exactly.'

THREE

'Are you sure about this?' Daniel muttered, a little later. Behind him, Sam stood twisting his cap in his huge hands. He looked like a caged bear next to Lady Clara, who was edging delicately away from him. He had the same bewildered, worried look as the poor dancing bear Lily had seen once when she and Henrietta were exploring the city. It was the only time she had come close to revealing her magic. She had wanted to heal the wretched creature, and tear apart the iron muzzle around its jaws. Instead she'd had to walk away feeling sick, with Henrietta trembling in her arms. Sam had that same air of helpless strength. He didn't want them to go, but he couldn't deny that the girls ought to be with family.

'We should go. My husband and Louis – your cousin, girls – will be expecting me for luncheon.'

'Now?' Sam growled, more bear-like than ever.

'Well, naturally,' Aunt Clara replied in a frosted voice.

'But the show – tonight… You haven't found anyone to replace us. Shouldn't we stay?' Georgie protested, and then her voice died away as Aunt Clara's magic spilled out over them. 'I suppose not…' she whispered.

'We can change it,' Daniel said dully. 'It doesn't matter. I'll go back to the original act. Until I can find someone else.'

'But you'll come back? Visiting?' Sam asked, and Lily caught his hand. Her own disappeared inside it.

'That would not be appropriate,' Aunt Clara snapped.

Lily looked up at him. She didn't even need magic to tell Sam silently that of course they would, appropriate or not. He nodded, the anxious creases round his eyes fading a little. 'You won't be too grand for us, then?' he whispered to her, and she rolled her eyes. 'We won't be staying,' she whispered back. 'But she might know where Father is. We have to try.'

Aunt Clara's coachman was waiting in her landau outside the theatre, wearing a thick uniform coat and a top hat, and looking hot. The horse, a beautiful grey with the shiniest of harnesses, looked bored, but he rolled a nervous eye towards Aunt Clara as she swept out of the theatre. Lily would almost have sworn he stood up straighter.

'She's like Mama, isn't she?' Georgie whispered, and Lily nodded. Their mother had terrified everyone at Merrythought. The whole house had been ruled by her moods. If she wanted quiet, the maids went about in stocking feet. It seemed that Aunt Clara ran her house on the same lines – but without magic.

The girls climbed into the carriage silently. They'd only lived at the theatre for a few weeks, but it felt more like home to Lily than Merrythought ever had, and she hated to leave. Daniel and Sam were on the front steps, with Maria, and some of the artistes. Aunt Clara had flinched visibly at the sight of them, but Lily and Georgie didn't care.

'I've packed for you,' Maria muttered, reaching up, and stuffing a battered carpetbag into Georgie's arms. She glared suspiciously at Aunt Clara, who stared through her, as if she simply couldn't see her. 'Just a few little things. To help you keep your end up with Madam Fancy.'

Henrietta barked loudly as the carriage trundled away – short, painful barks that made Lily's skin crawl. Henrietta couldn't do spells herself, but that noise came close to magic. The sad little crowd on the steps drew closer to each other, shivering, and Sam started forward, as though he meant to chase the carriage. The last Lily saw of them was Daniel pulling him back.

The theatre was out of sight now, however much she craned her neck around the hood of the carriage. Lily swallowed, staring down at the darned gloves Georgie had insisted she put on. They were beautifully mended, but they were more darn than glove. 'Aunt, how old is our cousin?' she asked, wanting to distract herself.

Aunt Clara frowned at her, and glanced meaningfully at the coachman. But then she seemed to decide that it was an innocent enough question.

'Louis is nine,' she answered. 'It will be pleasant for him to have companions close to his own age. Well-behaved companions,' she added, fixing Lily with a diamond stare.

Lily nodded, very slightly. She supposed that Louis didn't do magic either – or no more than Aunt Clara. How on earth did he stop himself? Of course their aunt wouldn't want her darling corrupted by his criminal cousins. 'What does –' she stopped, realising that she had no idea what their uncle was called. 'Your husband, Aunt Clara. What does he do?'

'Sir Oliver is a gentleman of leisure,' her aunt replied coldly. 'He has estates in the north. He comes of a very old family. Very respectable.'

Obviously not a magician then, Lily translated. So their cousin had only half magician blood. But still. Even the littlest magic usually travelled down the family line. Some magicians were stronger than others, of course. Lily had a much harder time controlling her magic than Georgie did, because Georgie simply didn't like the magic very much. She had been forced into using it in strange and unpleasant ways by their mother, and she'd had enough. Besides, if she let her magic spill out, the unknown spells Mama had planted inside her stirred, and odd, dangerous things began to happen. It was safer to pretend the magic wasn't there at all. It would be torture for Lily, but Georgie seemed to be able to stuff it away inside her and ignore it quite happily. Perhaps Louis was the same.

The coachman drew up in front of a grey stone house, with scrubbed-white steps leading up to the blackest, shiniest front door Lily had ever seen. It was not a friendly-looking house, and even in a street of smart stone houses, it gleamed a little more than the others. It was almost the stone version of Aunt Clara's spell, a monument to manners and good taste. As a footman hurried down the steps to assist them from the carriage, Lily felt as if an invisible thread had attached itself to her scalp, dragging her to stand up straight.

'I suppose it's hardly worth sending you to your rooms to change for lunch,' Aunt Clara sighed, twitching off her gloves. 'You're unlikely to have anything more suitable to change into. Very well. William, tell Cook we will have lunch now.'

The footman glided away, and Lily felt almost grateful for the invisible thread. Part of her wanted to huddle away quietly somewhere, but she set her shoulders back further, and looked around the entrance hall, trying to seem unimpressed.

It wasn't as big as Merrythought, of course, but it was *richer*. The footman had been crusted with gold braid, and there was even more of it on the dark velvet curtains. Daniel would have loved them for the theatre, Lily thought, smiling unhappily. Nothing was faded, or dusty. Even the ancient-looking portraits shone.

'You brought them.' The boy from the theatre was walking down the curved staircase, and Lily watched him curiously. The only other boy she knew well was the mute servant-boy at Merrythought, Peter. He had spiky brownish hair, and a mostly brownish face, tanned from working outdoors. Their cousin looked rather like him. A younger, well-fed, perfectly-groomed version, the brown hair neatly trimmed to sit above his snow-white shirt collar. His eyes were a hard blue, like Aunt Clara's – or like her glamour, anyway.

'These are your cousins.' Aunt Clara nodded, her voice slightly brittle.

She hates doing this, Lily realised. *Bringing us into her house, and endangering him. But she thinks we're more dangerous at the theatre. She can't risk us dishonouring her family all over again, if we're recognised.* Lily shivered as the choking magic of the house settled on her shoulders. *We mustn't stay here long. She may not be making spells on purpose any more, but her magic's all through this house already. It's going to squash us into perfect little ladies.*

Louis bowed politely, but he didn't smile, and Henrietta squirmed in Lily's arms. Lily could tell she didn't like him. She sighed inwardly. Henrietta was not a tactful dog. She would have to do her best to keep her and Louis away from each other.

They followed Aunt Clara to a red-painted dining room that made Lily think of raw meat. She wasn't hungry in the slightest, and she could feel Louis staring at her sideways.

A tall, thin man strode into the room, and stopped as soon as he saw Lily and Georgie. He peered at them through an eyeglass attached to his waistcoat, and Lily heard Louis snigger. 'I see you found our little – ah – relatives,' he said quietly.

'There's no doubt.' Aunt Clara sat down at the table,

waving Lily and Georgie into seats on the other side. Henrietta hid herself under the snowy tablecloth, glaring at Lily in a way that suggested she expected to be fed too.

'No, I see the resemblance. Dreadful clothes. We will have to engage a governess, I suppose.' He tucked the eyeglass away, and nodded once at Lily and Georgie, and then proceeded to ignore them for the rest of the meal.

Georgie was bowed over her plate, toying miserably with a portion of salmon. Lily could see how upset she was. She had made their dresses, with help from Maria.

Lily was more worried about the idea of a governess. She had never had one, of course, but she had a vague idea that governessing involved learning to speak Talish, and the art of conversation, and deportment – which was just another word for manners. None of it sounded in the slightest bit interesting. But the worst part was that if they were sent back to the schoolroom, they would be children again. After weeks of being treated as valued members of the theatre company, they were already being dismissed as unimportant little girls. Still, a governess would take time to engage, surely. Hopefully they would be gone before she arrived.

'Do you go to school?' Lily asked Louis, who was sitting across the table from her.

Aunt Clara and her husband – it was impossible to

think of him as Uncle Oliver, although she supposed he was – were discussing some issue with the servants, and Lily spoke in a low voice, not wanting to draw their attention. She had a feeling that her aunt didn't really want them to talk to Louis – or not without her listening, at least.

Louis gave her a fishlike look, as though he didn't expect girls to speak.

'I asked if you went to school,' Lily repeated, smiling sweetly at him. Stupid boy. Did he think if he ignored her she'd just go away?

He stared back at her with dislike. 'Of course I do. It's the holidays now. But you could hardly go there. It's a boarding school, and only for boys.'

Lily lifted her head a little, so as to glare down her nose at him. She supposed they had just arrived in his house with very little warning, but he had no need to be so rude.

It was only for a little while, she told herself. Until they could find out where their father's prison was. Lily had a sudden dismal thought: *And then what will we do?* The dull red of the walls seemed to be pressing in on her, squashing all their hopeful plans. Finding him was only the beginning. He was hardly likely to be able to mend Georgie from within a prison. They were going to have to get him out. Stealing someone from a secret magicians' jail sounded much more difficult here than it had back at the theatre.

Lily pushed her salmon around her plate. It was an odd colour, like the trapeze artists' flesh-coloured tights. She hid the rest of it under her cutlery, struck by a sudden wave of homesickness. They should have stayed.

A cold insistent nose pressed against her leg, and a little of the gloom lifted. Lily fumbled the bread roll off her side plate into her lap, and fed it to Henrietta, who sniffed disapprovingly. She'd been spoiled by the corners of meat pies she begged from Sam and the stagehands, and a mere roll wasn't what she was used to.

The lunch seemed to go on for ever, with Georgie sagging miserably beside her, and Louis sulking across the table. But eventually Aunt Clara rose, and beckoned the girls to follow her upstairs.

The house was dark, with heavy gilded wallpapers, and strangely quiet. Lily was sure that there were a great many servants, and here and there she thought she heard a footstep, but clearly they had been trained to keep out of their mistress's way.

'I have asked the housekeeper to prepare a room for you to share,' Aunt Clara told them as she trailed her mass of skirts over the polished wooden floors. 'As you were accustomed to share at—' Words seemed to fail her at the horror of it. 'Where you were before...'

'Thank you,' Lily murmured, admiring the room as their aunt opened the door. It was probably four times the size of their room at the theatre, and even their old bedrooms back at Merrythought would have fitted into it easily. She had wondered if they would be stuffed into some back corridor, being unfortunate relations, but perhaps she had been unfair to Aunt Clara.

'I will leave you to settle in. I must go and draft an advertisement for a governess. Sir Oliver is quite right. We can hardly bring you out into society without a little polish.'

'Bring us out into society?' Lily muttered as she closed the door. 'I don't want to be brought out! Like those stupid girls who came to see the show, all covered in lace and feathers every night? I'd rather go back to Mama.'

Georgie gasped, and Lily hunched her shoulders angrily. 'All right, so I wouldn't. But this house is horrible. It's so *cushiony*. I feel like I can hardly breathe.'

'The cushions are rather comfortable,' Henrietta reported from the velvet chaise longue under the window. 'I think your aunt's horror of magic has infected the whole house, though.' She snorted. 'It's almost funny. She's so frightened of magic, she's using more magic to try and shut it out. It's a wonder she's still sane enough to walk. It's dampening your power, though, this house. It'll be good practice for you, learning to work round it.'

'I suppose we just keep telling ourselves it's not for long,' Lily sighed.

Georgie sat down next to Henrietta, looking out of the window at the sunny street below. 'But I don't think she knows anything. She's forsworn magic. And we can hardly ask her anyway! She won't want to talk about her dreadful brother-in-law, will she? Father shamed her by being sent to prison. She said she hadn't spoken to Mama for over ten years – she must have broken the connection with our family when he was arrested.'

Lily curled up on the floor, leaning against the chaise longue, her cheek against Henrietta's smooth side. 'Actually, I wouldn't put it past Aunt Clara to have given evidence against him. It would have been the best way to prove she really wasn't a magician any more, wouldn't it? To betray one?'

Henrietta growled in disgust. 'If she laid information on your father, which I can well believe, then surely she must know where they're keeping him. She may even have had to go there to give evidence.'

'So we just have to get her to tell us.' Lily nodded determinedly.

*

It was all very well making that sort of decision, but they couldn't make Aunt Clara talk when they never saw her. The hours of a society lady were very different to those of her young nieces. It turned out that Aunt Clara breakfasted in bed, took luncheon only rarely, and dined at one grand party after another. Lily and Georgie heard from her by means of notes, slipped under the door of their room by a silent maid. A pile of etiquette books appeared on the little table of inlaid wood that stood by the chaise longue, with a note instructing them to practise before the arrival of their governess. And a wardrobeful of pretty, frilled, little-girlish dresses were delivered the day after they arrived. The maid who unpacked them was polite, but would only answer their eager questions with, 'I couldn't say, miss,' or 'No, indeed, miss.' It made Lily want to stamp on her foot.

The same maid – her name was Agnes – accompanied them on polite twice-daily walks in the park close by the house, walking behind them and carrying a black umbrella, in case it should be needed.

No one had told the girls that they ought to stay in their own quarters, but somehow it was hard to venture out, apart from meals – and even then, supper was served in their room, as their aunt and uncle were always dining away.

'I don't think I can bear this much longer,' Lily muttered, on the second day, flinging *Elegant Flowers of Conversation for the Young Miss* across the room.

'We could ring for Agnes. It's almost time for a walk,' Georgie suggested, smoothing out the fabric in her lap admiringly. A workbox had arrived with the books, along with a handbook on embroidery. Lily suspected that her sister was actually enjoying herself, which only made it worse.

'I don't want a walk!' she snapped. 'I want to go home. Oh, I mean the theatre,' she added crossly, as Georgie's eyes widened in fear. 'I never would go back to Merrythought and Mama, Georgie. I only said it that once because of this awful house. It's still squashing me.'

There was a scratching noise, and Lily stalked across the room to open the door for Henrietta. 'Where have you been?' she demanded, and the pug's ears flattened. She nudged the door shut with her nose, and then whirled round to glare at Lily.

'Exploring, as you should have been!' she snapped. 'You're letting this house turn you into a prisoner just like your father.'

'Fine.' Lily rattled the door open again, and strode out into the passage.

'Good, good.' Henrietta wagged her stubby curl of

a tail eagerly. 'Where shall we go?' she whispered, her eyes glinting.

Lily frowned. 'Where is Sir Oliver?' she asked.

'Lily, don't…' Georgie stood in the doorway, trailing her embroidery and looking worried.

'I only want to know where he is so as not to go there!' Lily rolled her eyes at her sister. 'I need to find where Aunt Clara keeps her papers. She may have letters. Something we can use to find out about Father.'

'But still… We shouldn't.'

'*You* aren't. And no one said we had to stay in this room.'

Georgie nodded reluctantly. It was true, but somehow it had been clear, even so. 'I should come with you.'

Lily shook her head. 'Why? It's easier to be quiet if there's only me. And Henrietta,' she added hurriedly, before the pug could take offence.

'Your aunt is out paying a call, and Sir Oliver is in his library, with the accounts,' Henrietta said smugly. 'I listened. There's a lot of big furniture in this house, I can hide behind it easily. And they like me in the kitchens. I've been doing tricks for them. And I caught a mouse in the scullery, so now the cook thinks I'm a treasure.'

'I wouldn't have thought a house as smart as this would have mice,' Lily said in surprise. 'Where would a mouse find to hide? Everything's so clean and polished.'

'It didn't have any.' Henrietta sat down, and scratched under her collar with a hind paw, gazing blissfully at the ceiling. 'Ahhh! Better. No, I had to go quite a way down the street to find one. And then the stupid thing got under the laundry copper, and made it very hard for me to capture it again.' She scratched again, and then shook herself irritably. 'And it *may* have given me a flea. Still. If we do run into any of the servants, just be polite, and say that I wanted to be let out. They won't mind.'

'You see?' Lily told Georgie. 'I'll be fine. I just need to go and explore a little, that's all. I can't bear being in here any longer. And once we have a governess, Georgie, there'll be someone watching us all the time. We need to nose around while we've got the chance.'

Georgie nodded reluctantly, and watched as Lily caught Henrietta up in her arms, and set off down the moss-green carpet.

It felt far more momentous than it ought to, Lily thought. She was only walking down a passageway! But after she'd been muffled up in that pretty, silken room for a day, even a passage felt exciting. 'Where are we going?' she whispered to Henrietta, pausing as they came to the balcony that ran around the entrance hall.

Henrietta's whiskers twitched. 'It's unfortunate that Sir Oliver is in the library,' she muttered. 'I suspect any

useful correspondence would be there. Although...
Your aunt has a little sitting room, attached to her
bedroom. That could be interesting.'

'How do you know all this?' Lily stared down at her.
'You haven't been out of our room that much.'

'I listen, Lily.' Henrietta laid her ears back irritably.
'Like I said, I've been in the kitchens, begging for sugar.'
She shuddered. 'I even let them balance biscuits on my
nose. It was most undignified. But I know that your aunt
has all the servants walking on tiptoe, they're so terrified
of her.'

'Why don't they just leave?' Lily drew back into the
shadow of a tall, broad-leafed plant, in a gilded stand. It
was large enough to shield them a little. The fat leaves
smelled of furniture polish, Lily noticed, shaking her
head slightly. Aunt Clara was even madder than Mama.

'She pays well. Very well, I think. His estates must be
rather large, and he has some sort of factory too. Your
aunt was lucky to catch him, especially with her
tarnished background.' Henrietta licked Lily's ear
lovingly. 'Stupid people. Your aunt most of all. It can't
be right to change oneself about like this. She has the
strangest smell, did you notice?'

Lily laughed, then put her hand over her mouth
quickly. 'No. I wish I could smell magic the way you do.
She feels strange when I'm close to her, though. I noticed

it most at that meal we ate, the first day we were here –
there's a sort of sweetness about her. It's in her voice,
and the glamour she wears, and it's all through the
house. I know it's all Sir Oliver's money, but this house
belongs to her, whoever's paying for it, and however
polite she is to him.'

'We could pretend we were looking for her,'
Henrietta suggested slyly. 'For you to ask about the
governess. Her sitting room is in the passage that
mirrors yours – off the other side of the balcony.'

'You're sure she's out?' Lily muttered, peeping out
around the plant. There was no one to be seen, but the
strange atmosphere of the house was making her
twitchy. It felt like someone was watching them.

'Quite sure.' Henrietta wriggled down from Lily's
arms, and trotted out on to the balcony, peering through
the balustrade and down to the empty main hall. Then
she looked back eagerly at Lily, and raced off, making
for the opposite passageway.

Lily followed her, padding along in the pretty little
kid slippers her aunt had provided. She probably hadn't
meant them for spying.

'Here.' Henrietta had stopped in front of a door.
'Knock on it,' she whispered.

'But she isn't here!' Lily frowned.

'Just make sure.' Henrietta rolled her marblelike

eyes. 'And if you knock, you can say you were looking for your aunt if anyone catches us. The servants here are very well-trained. Very quiet. Someone could be watching.' She glanced around, and shut her mouth uneasily, with a little snap of teeth.

Lily had her hand on the gilded door handle, when there was a tapping of feet across the marble floor of the hallway, and a murmur of voices at the front door.

'Aunt Clara's back!' Lily jumped away from the door as if it had bitten her, and raced back along the passageway to the balcony.

She could hear her aunt's voice in the hall now, asking the footman to send her maid to her room. Lily looked around her worriedly – her plan had been for no one to see her, however much she protested that they were allowed to explore. She put out her hand to a long velvet curtain draped around the window, thinking that perhaps she could duck behind it, when another hand closed over hers. Lily screamed – quietly – and tried to wrench her hand away.

'What are you doing sneaking around?' her cousin snapped, stepping out from behind the curtain.

'I wasn't! And what are you doing hiding behind curtains?' Lily gasped back. Her heart was still thudding so hard it felt as if parts might snap. She had looked down at the fingers round hers expecting them to be scaly, or at least clawlike, not just ink-stained and bitten-nailed.

'This is my house. I can sit where I like.' Louis was a year younger than Lily, but he was taller, and he looked down at her as if she were some sort of worm. 'You *were* sneaking. I saw you hovering outside my mother's room.'

Lily glanced down at Henrietta worriedly. They had been whispering, but he still might have been close enough to hear them. But he couldn't have done. He would have said something. Surely.

There was a whispering of silk skirts on the balcony, and Louis hurriedly let go of Lily.

Aunt Clara didn't so much as raise her eyebrows seeing the pair of them together. Only the slightest catch in her gliding step betrayed her surprise.

'Good afternoon, Aunt,' Lily stammered, wanting to say something before Louis accused her of spying. 'I was coming to find you. Georgie and I wanted to know if you had succeeded in finding us a governess.'

Aunt Clara looked down at her thoughtfully. 'I'm afraid not yet.' She walked around Lily, admiring her from all angles. 'You look very well indeed,' she murmured. 'And the dog too. Very pretty.'

Lily blushed. She wasn't used to compliments. She wondered if it was another part of her aunt's strange twisted magic, that suddenly her opinion seemed so important. Aunt Clara was still staring at her, and Lily fidgeted uneasily.

'I suppose it was naïve of me to expect you to stay quietly in your room,' her aunt said at last. 'It doesn't surprise me that it's you I find – shall we say exploring? To be polite about it? Unless your sister is wandering around some other part of the house?'

Lily shook her head. 'She's doing embroidery,' she muttered.

Aunt Clara nodded, as though she had thought as much. 'Quite.'

'She was spying!' Louis burst out.

'Well, of course she was!' Aunt Clara smiled lovingly at him. 'And so would you have been, dearest. Your cousin is a curious child, just like you.' She gave Lily a look of distaste. 'Not *quite* like you.'

'I haven't been…' Lily began, but Aunt Clara glared at her, clearly telling her to be silent.

Lily bit her bottom lip. Was it possible that Louis didn't know about his mother's magical background? Hadn't anything strange ever happened to him, something that made him wonder about his family? Lily looked at him thoughtfully. His mouse-brown hair was ruffled, and his clothes looked more dishevelled than when she'd seen him last. But he didn't look as though his breakfast had gone floating around the room, or his bed had sprouted paws recently. Lily's own magic had only started to work properly a few weeks before, and she was older than Louis. Perhaps nothing had happened to him yet. Perhaps he took after his father, and nothing ever would. Still, she thought Aunt Clara was taking a great risk, not warning him. What if he had inherited magic, and it suddenly exploded out of him one day?

'Come and sit with me, Lily,' Aunt Clara said sweetly. 'I want to talk to you.' She swished gracefully along the passage to her sitting room. Lily followed her, and Louis stared after them resentfully.

Aunt Clara's sitting room was as perfect as she was. There were a great many flowers, and the air was so heavy with their scent that Lily noticed every breath she took. She could even taste them, a honey sweetness on the back of her tongue. When Aunt Clara closed the door, the perfume wrapped Lily round, dizzying her, and she slumped into a delicate little chair, shaking her head. Henrietta was staggering, her delicate nose hit even harder than Lily's.

'Your manners are quite graceless,' her aunt told her disapprovingly. 'And you are shockingly indiscreet! You will not mention our family failings in this house, do you understand? Louis does not know about my family, and he must not. This is why I brought you here! I can't risk the secret getting out!' Her perfectly manicured nails were digging into her palms, and her eyes shone brilliantly.

'But shouldn't you tell him? Won't he be scared – if something happens?' Lily whispered, pulling Henrietta on to her lap. She put her hands across her face to protect herself from the flowers. 'And can't anyone see what you're doing? I don't understand. These flowers can't be real. It's a spell, it must be.' She peered at Aunt Clara over her fingers, trying to catch some hint of the woman behind the mask of glamour.

'Stupid child!' Aunt Clara snapped. 'The flowers are simply expensive! I doubt you've ever seen anything like them, shut away in that rotting old hulk of a house. I have given magic up, entirely, how many times do I need to explain it?'

Until you take the glamour off, Lily said to herself. But Aunt Clara really did seem to believe it herself.

'Aunt Clara,' she said suddenly. It wasn't the best time to ask about where her father might be, Lily felt, but she wasn't sure she'd have another opportunity. 'Do you know where Father is being held? Where the magicians' prison is?'

Aunt Clara quivered with horror. The crystal combs in her hair actually vibrated, Lily realised, and tiny sparks of something flickered around her aunt's hair. 'No, I do not! How would I know something like that? There is no magic in this house, child! No magicians!' She swallowed, bringing herself back under control with effort. 'Never ask me such things again. Now. If you can manage to behave like a young lady, I have a suggestion to make.' Aunt Clara's tone made it clear that it was actually more of an order.

Lily nodded faintly. She was getting used to the flowers now. Aunt Clara was right – she simply hadn't seen anything like them before. Even the bouquets that had been thrown on to the stage at the theatre were nothing to these. The white, waxy petals of the plant nearest her were jewelled with tiny drops of sweetness, to entice passing bees, Lily guessed. As Aunt Clara paced the room, looking away from them, Henrietta climbed on to the arm of the chair, and licked it delicately. 'Sugar!' she whispered delightedly.

'We are lucky enough to live next door to a very eminent man. One of the queen's own counsellors. His name is Jonathan Dysart.' She looked at Lily as though she expected her to recognise the name, but Lily shook her head. 'He really is extremely influential.' Aunt Clara sighed happily to herself. 'And he has two daughters. Twins, called Cora and Penelope.' She settled herself carefully on the chair opposite Lily's, and eyed her closely. 'Most unfortunately, they do not get on with Louis.'

Lily wasn't surprised. She didn't think anyone would. But then, it did give her a rather better opinion of her cousin. He was clearly able to stand up to Aunt Clara.

'It would be most convenient if you and Georgiana were to cultivate a friendship with Jonathan Dysart's daughters.' Aunt Clara was leaning forward now, and her hands were so closely grasped that her knuckles had whitened. What was so important about Jonathan Dysart? Lily wondered.

'What does he do?' she murmured.

Aunt Clara sighed. 'He is so very close to the queen. And to the Dowager – her mother, that is. I've always wanted... That is... To be associated with someone in those circles... There would be no suspicion of a taint any longer, I'm quite sure.'

'She's deranged,' Henrietta breathed in Lily's ear. 'Obsessed.'

Lily nodded. She was feeling rather more frightened of Aunt Clara now. Their aunt was so wound up with denying her own old magic. Clearly, she meant to make Lily and Georgie do the same. She was going to turn them into perfect, ordinary little society misses. Whatever it took.

'Don't let her get you alone,' Henrietta muttered.

'Especially not round anything sharp.'

Lily glared at her. A talking dog was bound to make Aunt Clara even more upset.

'I think it would be quite appropriate to invite Cora and Penelope to take tea with you and your sister,' Aunt Clara purred. 'Don't you?'

Lily nodded. She really didn't have a choice.

FOUR

unt Clara lost no time in sending a sweetly worded message to the children next door, and the visit was arranged for two days later. Lily was quite looking forward to it. The new governess had still not arrived, and she was fed up with all the etiquette books, and even more so with Georgie's calm embroidering.

'We have to make them like us,' Lily explained to her. 'Aunt Clara's certain that their father can make her friends with the queen – or something like that. And if their father's some sort of royal counsellor, maybe they might know things? Or they could find them out for us, perhaps. If we – made them…' She swallowed. The idea of putting a spell on someone to make them do what she wanted was exciting and horrible at the same time. 'No.

We mustn't. It's too dangerous, and Aunt Clara would have a fit if she found out.'

She didn't mention their aunt's worrying obsession with ridding their family of the taint. Perhaps when Aunt Clara had got her claws into Jonathan Dysart she wouldn't worry about it quite so much. At the moment, Lily had a feeling that their plans to rescue Father might push Aunt Clara even further into her strange, obsessive thoughts. And if they admitted that Georgie's magic had been turned into a weapon to assassinate the queen, Lily was convinced that her aunt would denounce them immediately. Lily sighed. She had to admit, that wasn't entirely unreasonable.

'I *know*, Lily,' Georgie said, in a long-suffering voice. 'You've explained it to me at least four times. Be nice to these girls. I will!'

'You didn't see what Aunt Clara was like,' Lily muttered. 'She's as frightening as Mama, Georgie; she just does it in a more honey-ish way.'

Georgie laid her embroidery over the sofa arm and pulled Lily down to sit beside her. 'Don't worry so much. All we have to do is charm two girls. It can't be that difficult. Do you think Aunt Clara would notice if you used just a very tiny spell?'

Lily shook her head. 'We'd better not risk it, though I wish we could. Besides, I'm not sure the house would let me do any spells. Aunt Clara hates magic so much, and that's seeped into everything. Even the furniture.' She shuddered. 'I feel like my skin's glowing all the time, there's so much magic tied up inside me.' She shrugged off Georgie's embrace, and stood up, pacing again. 'We should change. Aunt Clara was very clear. We need to make a good impression.'

Georgie shook her head, smiling, and Henrietta eyed Lily, with her nose even more deeply wrinkled than usual. 'You really want this to work,' she said thoughtfully.

Lily sighed. 'I want to get out of here, that's all. I'm still not convinced Aunt Clara doesn't know. And even if she doesn't, if we do as she says, we've more chance of being allowed out, haven't we? Into society. To talk to people.' She hurried over to the heavy, dark wood wardrobe in the corner of the room. She didn't much like the sort of silk dresses that Aunt Clara had provided for them both – too frilly – but she had to admit they were beautifully made, and Georgie had positively purred at the delicacy of the stitching. She'd spent ages cooing over the cobwebby lace on the upstanding collars of the ones that were clearly meant to be best dresses. They were far nicer than anything the girls had had at Merrythought. Lily had always had Georgie's hand-me-downs anyway, although her sister hadn't been hard on clothes, as she'd spent all her time studying her magic lessons with Mama.

As Lily hauled the dresses out, Georgie jumped up crossly. 'Lily! Not like that. Be careful. You'll catch the trimming.'

'It wouldn't be hard,' Lily muttered. These dresses were in a style more like Aunt Clara's own, though only knee-length, instead of sweeping the floor like their aunt's. The tight bodices flared into five layers of flounces, and they had pads at the back to make the skirts stick up, and then more skirt drawn back and tied in enormous bows over the bustle pads.

'I feel twice the size of me!' Lily hissed irritably, as Georgie did up the line of tiny buttons down the back of the bodice. 'And how am I ever supposed to get out of it again?'

'I like it,' Henrietta told her approvingly. 'Very proper. Very ladylike. Arabel had pretty dresses, though she spoilt them regularly. She had a very good mending spell in the end.'

'I can't even move my arms with these stupid sleeves,' Lily growled, flapping a little, to squish the big puffy bits at her shoulders.

'Don't do that!' It was Georgie and Henrietta together, and they exchanged a disgusted glance. It was probably the most in sympathy they'd ever been, Lily realised, smiling a little in spite of the ridiculous dress. She knew it was fashionable, beautiful even, but it just didn't feel like her. The colour particularly – she didn't feel right in the pale ice blue.

Clumsily, she buttoned Georgie into her pink version of the dress, and they glanced at the door. 'The drawing room, then?' Lily said, and Georgie followed her, padding out into the passageway in their pretty soft leather boots.

The drawing room was gold and white, and full of mirrors. It made the room beautifully light, but somehow cold. Lily shivered as they sat on a white brocade sofa, waiting for the other girls to arrive. The strange atmosphere of the house was no easier to live with now that they were allowed out of their room. She felt as though the many mirrors were reflecting her back and forth between them, thinning her out every time, so that she was a washed and shrunken child, who could be made to do whatever she was told.

The door rattled, and she jumped in panic, startling Georgie into a nervous laugh. Henrietta growled, and twitched.

Aunt Clara swept in silkily, smiling in approval at their pretty dresses, and the ribbons Georgie had tied in their hair. 'Good. Very good. I shall tell Fraser to serve tea at four.'

Lily nodded. The delicate golden sunburst clock on the mantelpiece said it was only half past three now. What were they supposed to do with these girls until tea arrived? It was all very well for Aunt Clara to say entertain them, but how? Neither Lily nor Georgie had ever paid or received a formal call, and the only girls they knew were each other – and Lydia, the jealous child star who had tried to sabotage Daniel's illusionist act, and denounce them to the Queen's Men.

'Aunt Clara…' Lily began, but the door swung open again, and Fraser announced, 'Miss Penelope Dysart, Miss Cora Dysart.' Aunt Clara hurried across the room in a flurry of silken flounces to kiss the visitors, and lead them fussily to Lily and Georgie.

'Do we curtsey?' Lily hissed, half to Georgie and half to Henrietta, who was just as likely to know.

'I'm not sure…'

'Shake hands!' Henrietta snarled back, rolling her eyes.

The four girls greeted each other uncomfortably, and Lily noted with horror that although Fraser had introduced the Dysart girls, she had no idea which was which – Cora and Penelope appeared to be identical twins. They were even dressed identically, in ruffled pale green dresses that matched their pale green eyes. They had the darkest hair Lily had even seen, and they wore it loose, cascading in curls down their backs.

'Good afternoon,' they said sweetly, together, and Lily shivered a little. Was it only the odd echoing effect of the girls speaking at once, or was there something strange in those voices?

Henrietta glanced up at her meaningfully, and Lily swallowed. The Dysarts were meant to be Aunt Clara's way of wiping out the nasty streak of magic that was spoiling her family's prospects. But they were as magical as she was trying not to be.

Lily tried to smile politely, but Penelope and Cora were watching her, their green eyes hard and mirror-like. They knew quite well that they had been recognised.

Aunt Clara was talking, a gentle stream of conversation on how lovely it was to have her dear nieces to stay, how much she had enjoyed girlish company, and ordering their dresses. But Lily knew that all of the girls wanted nothing more than for her to leave – so they could talk properly.

Georgie didn't play a part in it, but Lily felt her magic coiling excitedly inside her, spreading out to meet the spell that was hazing the air of the drawing room, sparkling in all the mirrors. The house couldn't fight off the power of three young magicians, she realised. And Aunt Clara was so happy the Dysart girls were here – she'd let her guard down.

The spell felt intriguingly different to one of her own, perhaps because of its dual nature – the twins had cast it together, she thought. It seized her magic hungrily, and she snatched it back, paying it out with care, like the crabbing lines she'd used with Peter, off the boathouse jetty. All three girls swirled their magic around Aunt Clara, telling her very firmly to leave. Lily shivered happily, and her magic purred inside her, glad to be set free. It was exciting, to be part of someone else's spell. But she wasn't stupid, and the Dysart girls' spell had dug in little hooked claws. She could feel them, pulling and testing and trying and stealing.

The pale green girls smiled at her sweetly – with not a hint of apology. Lily smiled a thin-lipped grimace back, and Georgie blinked anxiously between them.

Aunt Clara stood up, and murmured something incoherent, something to do with seeing about the fish. Then she walked out of the room, with a slight list to one side, as though she wasn't entirely in control of her own feet.

'Thank goodness she's gone.'

'I quite despise your aunt.'

Cora and Penelope spoke at the same time, and Lily found it hard to separate out their humming voices.

'Such a waste of talent – only a minor one, admittedly, but she could be so much better if she tried.'

'She's quite good at her glamour,' Lily pointed out. It felt odd, defending Aunt Clara when she couldn't stand her either, but Aunt Clara was theirs. She wasn't going to let a pair of strangers insult her. Not yet, anyway.

'That!' One of them sniffed. 'Only because she's been using it so long she's forgotten she does it. I'm sure she thinks she's completely natural.' They sniggered, together.

'There's a deadening spell on the house too,' the other one said, shaking her dark curls irritably. 'It makes my ears buzz. Anyway. None of that matters. Who are you two? And why are you here? We only came because our father said we must, that the dreadful Fish woman wouldn't let up until we did. And we were mildly interested to meet you.'

Lily was certain they had been. She could just imagine what fun these two would have with a pair of non-magical sisters living next door.

'What on earth is the Fish doing, having you here? She can't stand magic, it's obvious. Doesn't she know what you are?'

Lily shrugged, elbowing Georgie in the silken flounces, to remind her sister that she was actually capable of talking.

'She thinks she can hide us better here, that's all,' she explained. 'She didn't even know we existed, until she met us by chance, and recognised us. Georgie resembles our mother, you see. Aunt Clara's sister.' She decided not to mention the theatre. Something about the icy perfection of the twins made her think that they would disapprove. It wasn't that Lily was ashamed – or so she told herself, very firmly. But she felt she needed every advantage she had in this little game.

'Your magic is a great deal stronger than your aunt's. I'm Penelope, by the way; I can see that you can't remember.'

Lily smiled, refusing to apologise. 'Thank you.' The remnants of the tussle over the spell to banish Aunt Clara were still floating about so powerfully that she could borrow a little of the girls' own magic. One dark lock of hair crawled slowly into the shape of a P, lying flat against Penelope's shoulder. Lily could feel Henrietta shaking with amusement, pressed up next to her ankle. Penelope didn't seem to notice – perhaps she just didn't think anyone would dare use a spell on her.

'Aunt Clara's spent so long trying to pretend she hasn't got any magic that she's almost spelled it out of herself. I expect she was a lot stronger once. The spell on this house is horrible.'

'She didn't tell our father your surname,' Cora put in, staring at Lily and Georgie curiously still.

Lily swallowed. It felt important – admitting who

they were to another magician. Aunt Clara had already known, or almost. She wondered if Cora and Penelope would have heard of Merrythought.

'I'm Lily Powers,' she said, trying not to sound either too proud or too apologetic.

'Georgiana Powers,' Georgie admitted.

Cora and Penelope looked slightly less than certain of themselves for the first time since they'd arrived. 'The Merrythought girls?' Cora asked, with almost a snap.

Lily nodded, holding back a smile. She felt absurdly pleased that the Dysarts had heard of them. But then, Daniel had known about Merrythought too. She should have expected it. And she had never heard of a family of magicians called Dysart – still, she and Georgie hadn't been very well educated.

Cora and Penelope were looking at each other, the glassy shallowness of their green eyes spoilt a little. They were most definitely rattled, Lily realised, watching them. She was trying to think how to ask what they knew about her and Georgie, when Penelope spoke, some of the sweet humming tone missing from her voice this time. 'We've heard of you.'

'Oh. Really?' Lily raised a polite eyebrow, the way Aunt Clara did when she wanted to make them feel particularly graceless.

'Your mother, more than you, actually.'

Lily swallowed. There seemed to be a strange frightened lump stuck inside her somewhere, so she could hardly get any words out. 'Oh?' she managed. She was impressed with how calm she sounded, and it seemed the Dysarts were too. They glanced at each other, and she could feel their magic, more tentative this time – soft, silky-stroking fingers instead of claws. She tried not to flinch as they played around her hair, tiny wisps of magic stealing into her with every breath.

'And your father is, ah…' Cora smirked sweetly at Penelope. 'Detained?'

Lily glared at her. 'Unfortunately,' she admitted coldly. Then, much as she hated asking these girls for a favour, she forced herself to smile a little, despite the fear inside her. 'We'd like to find him…'

Penelope and Cora snorted in unison, a delicate, ladylike little noise, that wonderfully expressed how stupid Lily was being.

'Well, that isn't going to happen, is it?' Cora purred.

Lily gritted her teeth. 'You don't know where he might be?' she pressed.

'No,' Penelope said flatly. 'Of course not. No one knows.'

Even with all her magic, Lily couldn't tell if the girl was lying. But it was obvious that the Dysarts either couldn't, or wouldn't, tell them anything useful. Lily's shoulders sagged. If Aunt Clara knew nothing, and neither did these two, what was the point of being here? They should just have stayed at the theatre.

No. If the Dysarts knew something about Mama, Lily and Georgie needed to find out exactly what. Lily flinched, feeling the twins' magic coiling around her in soft, sticky strands.

Georgie batted her hands across her face, and frowned. 'You could just ask whatever it is, instead of spying.'

Lily stared at her, and Georgie shrugged. 'Well, that's what they're doing. Why don't they just come out with it? We all know what we are.'

Lily nodded, her eyes still wide. Every so often Georgie surprised her with a return to the confident, loving older sister she had been before Mama's magic lessons crushed her. Perhaps a day of quiet embroidery had restored her spirits a little.

'Then you are part of it too. We thought so.' Cora nodded in satisfaction. 'Not that you'll manage it, you know. You can see how strong we are. We're going to be the ones to get rid of her. It might take us a year or so more, but we *shall* do it. Everyone says so.'

The fearful lump was growing, and Lily felt she could hardly breathe through it now. Georgie had seized her hand, and her nails were digging into Lily's fingers, hard enough to hurt. Lily knew they must be hurting, but she couldn't feel them at all.

How very strange, was all she could think. *They actually want it to happen. We ran away from Mama, and our home. We ran away to nowhere with a couple of dresses each, and a painted dog, and a bag of stolen gold. And they're boasting about the same plot we're trying to outrun.*

She coughed, squashing the fright away somewhere. It would come back later, she was sure, but for now she smiled. She felt Henrietta nip Georgie's fingers to make her let go. Dull half-moons of pain were rising on the back of her hand, and it helped to clear her head. Hopefully Penelope and Cora would think she was only frightened they were going to win.

'Do they really?' she asked, widening the smile a little as the thoughts buzzed anxiously inside her. Everyone says so? *Everyone?* How many people were involved in this plot? They had vaguely known that other magician children were working to restore magic to the country, but Lily had always imagined they were hidden away in remote corners, as she and Georgie had been. Cora and Penelope were as unhidden as they could possibly be, and it sounded as though there were a circle of magicians around them, too.

Lily wondered just how they were planning to assassinate Queen Sophia. She didn't think they had spells implanted deep inside them, as Georgie had. There was no need, when they obviously knew exactly what they were supposed to do, and were rather looking forward to it. There was an identical expression of slight annoyance on their faces now, as though the girls weren't used to being doubted. Lily could feel the magic seething inside them. As though they were preparing to prove exactly how good they were...

It was probably lucky that Fraser opened the door to usher in a trio of footmen with silver trays of tea, and cake, and very delicate sandwiches.

The four girls sat staring frostily at each other, while the footmen moved spindly little tables, and unloaded trays. There was very little magic that could be done while holding a plate of cucumber sandwiches, Lily thought gratefully.

Eventually, the footmen marched out again, and Fraser closed the door behind him with a velvet thump.

'Your aunt is desperately vulgar, but she serves good cake,' Penelope murmured, after a little while.

Lily nodded, although she didn't really know. She could hardly taste the food. She was waiting for one of them to fling something at her, perhaps a fireball, like the one Georgie had thrown at Daniel, the first time they met. Aunt Clara would blame her if it singed the curtains, Lily thought vaguely.

But it seemed that the Dysart girls had decided it would be impolite to nobble the competition in their own house. Or perhaps they thought that Lily and Georgie might be stronger on their own territory. They finished their tea with only occasional delicate spells floating across the room, most of which Lily and Georgie ignored. The flower arrangements became more voluptuous, and grew several odd additions, as spells were deflected into them, and at one point the sunburst clock melted slightly. That was Lily's fault, as she was wondering how much longer the Dysarts could possibly stay.

Then, with an amused glance at the seeping clock, Cora rose, and bowed a little. 'So very pleasant to meet you. You will call on us, won't you? It's so lovely to have company next door – such very *nice* company.'

Lily nodded, and Georgie murmured, 'Of course,' and rang for Fraser.

As he ushered Cora and Penelope out, Lily sank back against the brocade of the sofa, and moaned.

Henrietta jumped up beside her. 'What on earth are you going to tell your aunt?'

FIVE

'What have you done to my mother?'

The drawing-room door swung open with a bang, and Lily jumped up like a cornered cat. Penelope and Cora had left her nervous, and the door slamming into the wall like that was the loudest noise the girls had heard in this house. Aunt Clara's spell usually seemed to muffle everything.

'Nothing!' Lily gasped, as her cousin snarled at her. 'I mean, what are you talking about?'

'She didn't even see me! I was talking to her, and she didn't know who I was. She just said something about trout.' Louis was hissing with anger, but his eyes were frightened.

Lily glanced helplessly at Georgie. What should they

say? Aunt Clara had been so determined that Louis wasn't to know about the magic. 'She – er – went off to lie down, while the Dysart girls were here visiting. Perhaps she isn't feeling well?' she suggested. She wondered how long Aunt Clara would keep talking about fish – Penelope and Cora had obviously included their nickname for her in the spell somehow.

'Them… I might have known.' Louis looked behind him, and obviously saw one of the servants lurking, for he closed the door quickly. 'You're like them, aren't you? *You* are, anyway,' he added, nodding to Lily.

'What are you talking about?' Lily repeated feebly. He wasn't supposed to know any of this…

'They're tainted. Magic-tainted, I'm sure of it. I can't prove anything, that's all. And no one would believe me.'

That awful word again. It wasn't a taint. Lily seethed silently. But how did he know?

'I can tell,' he muttered, leaning back against the door, looking lost. 'They feel strange, and so do you. All wrong.'

'He does have some magic in him then,' Georgie muttered in her ear. 'Or he wouldn't notice.'

'Not very much.' Lily sniffed. 'Strange how?' she demanded.

He shrugged. 'Just strange. You've got it, haven't

you? Mama's always trying to see if I have too, it runs in her family.'

Lily nodded. She still disliked Louis, but he was suddenly a great deal more interesting. 'She thinks you don't know anything about it,' she murmured, watching him carefully.

Louis grunted in disgust. 'I'm not stupid.' He shivered suddenly. 'I wish I didn't know. Every morning I wake up thinking it'll be today when it happens.'

Lily nodded. She'd felt the same – only she had been desperately wishing for the magic to come, not dreading it. 'You might like it.'

Louis stared up at her through his tangled fringe. 'Are you mad?' he demanded coldly. 'I don't want to be shut up in Fell Hall, even if you do!'

'Fell Hall?' Lily echoed. Then she gasped, and ran across the room, seizing his hands. 'Is that the prison? The magicians' prison? Do you know where it is?'

Louis pushed her away. 'Don't you know anything?' he snapped, dusting down his sleeves, as though he were exquisitely dressed, and Lily had fatally crumpled a perfect outfit. 'Of course it isn't a prison. No one knows where the magicians' prison is.' He hesitated, and added miserably, 'Although I suppose Fell Hall probably feels like one, when you're there. It's a school. A reform school, for the children of magicians.'

'Like us…?' Georgie asked, her voice very small.

Louis didn't even bother answering her. 'I don't understand why those snakes from next door aren't there,' he muttered. 'If anyone needs reforming, it's them.'

'Too well-connected,' Lily pointed out. 'That's why they were here. For us to get on their good side.'

'Did you?' Louis asked suspiciously.

'I don't think so. They – er—' Lily wasn't quite sure what to tell him. It obviously wasn't safe to mention the plot. 'They seemed worried that our magic might be as strong as theirs,' she admitted.

'But it isn't, because we don't actually do any. Of course,' Georgie put in hurriedly.

Louis snorted.

'We really haven't done any magic in this house,' Lily told him. It was only a very little bit of a lie.

'So you could? If you wanted?' he asked, peering at her, round-eyed.

'If we were doing magic here, our first spell would be to teach you some manners,' Henrietta remarked calmly from the sofa. 'You've been remarkably rude, ever since we arrived.'

Louis gawped at her for a few seconds, and then drew himself up straight. 'I knew there was something unnatural about you,' he told her, trying not to sound scared.

'Magic is perfectly natural.' Henrietta smirked at him. 'It's denying it that's wrong. You'll come to a bad end, if you try to hide it.'

'And I'll be shut up in a school full of freaks if I don't!' he snapped back. 'Besides, I might not have any magic. I probably won't. Mama doesn't. What?' He glared at Henrietta and the girls as they all began to laugh.

'Her bad end is taking rather a long time to arrive, that's all...' Henrietta explained. 'She has been denying her magic for years, except for a few spells she has on this house, and herself. She has a remarkably determined way of looking at things, it seems to me. She thinks the spells are just her high standards, and society manners, but it's far more than that. And they're grown into her now. She'll never be rid of them.'

'She doesn't...' Louis faltered, as he seemed to realise what he was saying – and what he'd been seeing, ever since he'd been old enough to understand. 'She just doesn't,' he muttered again. But the girls could tell he knew, deep down. He was silent for a moment, staring unseeingly at the melted clock, and then he seemed to harden, shaking off his fear, and looking sharply at Lily. 'Why did you think Fell Hall was a prison? What do you want to know about prisons for?'

'Our father is in one.'

'A gaolbird! Does Mama know?' Louis's eyes brightened at the thought of scandal. 'She'd have a fit.' He almost giggled, as if he was so scared he'd turned silly.

'She probably put him there,' Lily told him bitterly. 'He wouldn't give up his magic. She would have been desperate to get him out of the way, wouldn't she?'

Louis nodded. 'She would only have been doing her duty as an Englishwoman,' he murmured, but he seemed uncertain about it. 'Family…' He shrugged. 'Her sister's husband, though, she ought not to have done it.'

'She would have been protecting her good name – and yours,' Henrietta told him sternly. 'Should she care more for her sister's family, or her own?'

'You can't defend her!' Lily protested, staring at Henrietta in surprise.

'I may not agree with her, but that's not to say I can't understand her reasoning.' Henrietta yawned, so widely that the ridged underside of her jaw glinted in the sunny drawing room. She shut her mouth with a snap, and looked sideways at Lily. 'Water under the bridge, now, anyway.'

'I suppose.' Lily sighed.

Louis glanced up, and then left the doorway, and came to crouch by Henrietta on the sofa. He clearly didn't dare touch her, but she darted out her purplish tongue, and licked his hand, so he squeaked with surprise, and smiled shyly. 'Mama won't let me have a dog. She says it wouldn't be fair, since I'm away at school for most of the time. She's right, but I would so love one.'

'Rude, but essentially good-natured,' Henrietta pronounced, licking him again. 'Like most boys.'

'I'm sorry – if she did betray your father.' Louis ventured to run a finger down Henrietta's velvet back.

'It's why we agreed to come here. Your mother thinks we want to be respectable, and come out into society – she can't imagine that anyone wouldn't want that.' Lily grimaced. 'But actually, we were hoping that she might know where Father is. That we might be able to find out. Are you sure Fell Hall isn't a prison as well as a school?' she asked hopefully.

Louis frowned. 'I don't know for certain, but I think the prison is somewhere different, from the things that Mama's said. It's a deep secret.' He eyed Lily and Georgie uncomfortably. 'That's why people never come out,' he added, his voice suddenly more gentle.

Lily blinked. 'What do you mean?'

'Well, then they'd know the secrets, wouldn't they?'

'Oh.' Lily stared at her hands. Ever since they'd left Merrythought, the way ahead had seemed to grow harder and harder. 'He doesn't have to get out by himself,' she said in a small voice. 'We're going to rescue him.'

Louis looked as though he wanted to snort with laughter, but for once he was being kind. 'You don't even know where it is,' he reminded her. 'And you can't really go asking, can you?'

Georgie frowned. 'We could ask those children at Fell Hall.'

They stared at her, and she shrugged.

'Well, they're the only other people we know about who've been using magic. That's why they've been sent there. Cora and Penelope would rather cut their noses off than tell us anything useful, that's obvious. They don't want Father out of prison, and helping us, do they? But I don't see why the children at Fell Hall wouldn't tell us. We could go there, and ask them.' She swallowed. 'After all, most of their parents are probably in the same prison as Father is.'

Lily gazed at her admiringly, and Georgie looked pleased with herself.

'Have you ever been to Fell Hall?' she asked Louis curiously. 'You sound like you know a lot about it.'

'No! Of course not. But people do talk about it sometimes. There was a boy at my school – he was always a little odd. He hardly spoke. Then after one Christmas, he never came back. They sent him there, everyone said so. We spoke about it afterwards, only a little, and out of hearing of the masters, of course. And one of the older boys came from Derbyshire, not so far away from Fell Hall. His nursemaid's family were employed there. He used to beg her to tell him stories about it, in the firelight, like ghost stories. They use strange medicines, she told him, and enchantments too, so the children are quiet, and can't make any terrible spells.'

'But they wouldn't do that.' Lily shook her head. 'Magic is illegal – that's why the children are there! How can they use magic to stop them doing any? That's just stupid.' *But it's just what Aunt Clara's been doing*, she added to herself.

Louis sighed, and shrugged. 'Perhaps these people are above the law. If they work for the queen…'

'It still doesn't seem right.' Lily frowned. 'How can the rules be different for the Queen's Men? It isn't fair.'

Louis shook his head. 'If your father was trying to overthrow the queen – and I'm not saying he actually was, so don't look at me like that,' he added, catching Lily's glare, 'how would the authorities stop him, a powerful magician, if they couldn't fight his magic with any of their own?'

Lily stared at him angrily. She could see that what he said made sense, in a way. But it still didn't make it feel right.

She was searching for the words to argue, when Georgie jumped up, flinging herself at the window – nearly knocking over one of the flower arrangements that had suffered in the battle between Lily and the Dysart girls.

'What is it?' Lily demanded anxiously. Georgie was standing with her hands pressed up against the window, peering out.

'That was Maria! I saw Maria!'

'Maria from the theatre?' Lily asked doubtfully.

'Yes,' Georgie snapped impatiently. She ran out into the panelled hall, and started to pull frantically at the heavy door locks. 'Help me open it!' she gasped to Lily. 'She was just walking away past the window. She must have tried to come and see us. I didn't hear anyone ringing the bell, did you?'

'Because she didn't.' Lily crouched down, picking up a folded screw of paper that had been pushed underneath the door. 'Look. She left a note.'

Georgie snatched at it eagerly, and Lily let her take the tattered paper. Georgie had loved Maria, and the companionship of the girls in the theatre wardrobe. She missed her, Lily knew.

'She's only written a line or two,' Georgie said disappointedly. 'There's another letter inside – she was only passing it on. Daniel asked her to bring it, as she was going to visit her sister.' She opened out the note, and another tightly folded letter dropped into her hands. 'It's for you.' She passed it curiously to Lily. 'Who on earth would be writing to you at the theatre? No one even knew we were there.'

Lily was staring at the letter, the familiar writing blurred with sudden tears.

'Lily, what is it?' Georgie asked worriedly. 'Who's written to you?'

Lily swallowed. 'Peter.' Fumbling, she tore at the sealed paper. 'He addressed it to Miss Lily, at the theatre. He must have known not to write our surname.'

'Who's Peter?' Louis muttered to Georgie.

'The kitchen boy, back at Merrythought,' Georgie murmured back, watching Lily scan the letter. 'He's a mute. He was abandoned…'

'Abandoned on an island full of witches?' Louis sounded shocked.

Georgie shrugged. 'Perhaps when he never spoke, they thought he had magic in him too. Lily, what does it say?'

'Merrythought was raided,' Lily told her quietly. She sat down, rather suddenly, on one of the uncomfortable little velvet chairs that were scattered around the entrance hall. 'The Queen's Men.'

'What?' Georgie snatched the letter. 'What happened? Where is Mama?'

'She fled…' Lily sighed. 'All we know is, she isn't *there*. She could be anywhere, Georgie.'

'I don't believe it.' Georgie looked up from the letter, staring at Lily. 'They're taking him to Fell Hall!'

'I thought you said he was a kitchen boy?' Louis frowned.

'He is.' Lily shook her head disgustedly. 'They're getting desperate. Or panicking, maybe. Perhaps someone got wind of the plot. Peter hasn't a shred of magic in him, anywhere.'

'They think he might have been corrupted – by association with us!' Georgie laughed bitterly. 'I'm surprised they haven't imprisoned all of the servants.' She shivered. 'Maybe they have… Except he must have got this letter to one of them, as they were taking him, so there's someone left, at least. How funny that he saw our picture in Mr Francis's newspaper.'

Lily smiled, rather miserably, and stroked Henrietta's soft black head. 'He recognised you,' she told the dog. 'It didn't look at all like us, but he recognised you. We shouldn't have worried about the newspaper picture, after all. He'd never have known where we were, if it wasn't for that.' She straightened her shoulders. 'Well, now we know what we have to do.'

Georgie blinked at her, and Lily hissed through her teeth, 'We have to go to Fell Hall, *now*, to get him back.'

'Oh…' Georgie nodded.

'But he's only…' Louis started to say it, but faltered as both the girls glared at him.

'He helped us to escape from Merrythought,' Lily told him. 'It's our turn to rescue him now.'

Louis nodded. 'I suppose you were going anyway.' He wrinkled his nose. 'How are you going to get to Derbyshire?'

Lily looked at Georgie doubtfully. 'We have a little money. We earned wages at the theatre. Perhaps a train? We've proper clothes now, young lady clothes. What was the name of the boy at your school who lived close to Fell Hall? We could say we're visiting his family, if anyone asked us.'

Louis chewed his lip. 'Tarrant,' he said at last, reluctantly. 'They live at a place called Blackwater House. I suppose it would work. Father has a railway almanac in his study. You could find the nearest station. Then you'd have to find a carriage to hire.'

'Or we could walk,' Lily pointed out. 'We might not get far trying to hire a carriage to Fell Hall. I shouldn't think they have many visitors.'

Louis nodded uncertainly. Lily wondered if he ever got to walk anywhere, other than the pretty park nearby. He was so sheltered, even if he did go to school. But she wasn't jealous, she realised in surprise. She would far rather live their ramshackle life at the theatre, or even have the strange old times at Merrythought back, than be suffocated in silk and velvet here.

'So we need to find your father's railway almanac,' Lily said, hoping that Louis might volunteer to help. He didn't.

'It'll be in his study,' was all he said, and then he retreated to the drawing-room door. 'Just don't do anything else to Mama. Or I'll tell – someone…'

Sir Oliver stayed closeted in his study all that night. He and Aunt Clara were supposed to have gone to some political dinner, but Aunt Clara had been laid low by what she called a 'slight headache'. She had also had words with the cook, forbidding her from serving fish, ever again. Even salmon.

After breakfast the next morning, Lily, Georgie and Henrietta crept out into the passageway. Georgie had the sewing box with her, for protection.

'What are you going to do with that?' Lily asked her irritably. She hadn't slept well, for worrying about Peter, and about her father too. If the Queen's Men were becoming fiercer, and more ruthless, what did that mean for him?

Georgie rolled her eyes. 'We need an excuse. I've used up all the embroidery floss. I'm going to ask

Aunt Clara if I may have some more.'

'But we're going to Sir Oliver's study. She won't be there.'

'I know that, but I'm perfectly capable of pretending that I don't. Sir Oliver thinks we're stupid anyway. We just have to act, Lily! We did enough pretending to be princesses of the Northern Wastes at the theatre, just make use of it!'

Lily sighed, and nodded. 'He ought to have gone out to walk around the park anyway.'

Henrietta nodded. 'He always does after breakfast. They said so in the kitchens.' She licked her chops appreciatively, thinking of the remnants of Sir Oliver's kidneys and bacon that she'd been treated to that morning.

The girls scurried across the entrance hall, and disappeared into the darker, panelled passage that housed the study, and the billiard room.

'He isn't there,' Henrietta promised, sniffing thoroughly at the study door. 'I'm quite certain. One can tell him by those disgusting cigars.'

Lily turned the door handle, which was so well-oiled it didn't even squeak, and they slipped into the room. It was high-ceilinged, but somehow still dark and cave-like, heavy velvet curtains half-obscuring the windows, and the furniture hulking and ugly.

'I don't think he let Aunt Clara decorate in here,' Georgie muttered.

'Where would a railway almanac be?' Lily asked, ignoring her.

Henrietta leaped up on to the desk chair, and went sniffing through the papers. 'He must write a great many letters,' she commented, dislodging a sheet of stamps, which went fluttering to the floor.

'Be careful,' Lily whispered crossly. 'We don't want him to know we were here.' She stooped to pick up the stamps, dull little reddish squares, printed with the queen's face. She looked a great deal younger than she had for real, driving past in that carriage, a few weeks back. Lily had felt sorry for her then – she'd seemed so brave and tired. But that was before she had heard about Fell Hall, and before the Queen's Men had stolen her friend. The sheet of stamps shook in her fingers, and Georgie put a hand on her arm. 'Don't tear them! Then he really would know we've been here.'

'I'd like to,' Lily nearly spat. 'And worse. I hate the queen!'

'You see, sir?' a sad, sweet little voice spoke from the doorway, and Lily turned slowly to look over her shoulder.

Cora Dysart was standing by the half-open door, looking tragically up at a red-faced man in a dark uniform. The uniform they had seen at the theatre, when the Queen's Men came visiting. Behind Cora was her sister, with another man who looked so like them he had to be their father. Jonathan Dysart, the counsellor to the queen. The hidden magician.

'We were so shocked by the things they said yesterday.' Cora shook her head tragically. 'Of course, so many people know that our family were once magicians – I suppose they thought we would be in sympathy!' She sobbed, and leaned against her father's arm. Only the girls in the study could see the malicious glint of her pale green eyes. 'I've never been so grateful that we escaped the curse of our family's blood!'

Penelope nodded, and shuddered, her hair falling forward. Lily saw that the curl she had bespelled was still there, coiled into a P. As she watched, Penelope tugged at it, and scowled as it sprang back into place.

She should have taken the spell off before they left, Lily realised dully. She had been stupid, leaving it for them to find. She felt rather pleased that they hadn't been able to remove her little charm – but that was probably why the Dysarts had decided to betray them. If they couldn't take off Lily's spell, it meant she was stronger than they were. And instead of fighting her, or racing her and Georgie to carry out the plot, they'd decided to let someone else do the work.

It was really rather clever.

SIX

Lily swirled and swam and floated, wisps of pale green coiling around her, and tugging her back up to the surface again.

She wasn't swimming. She was lying on a bed, and the bed was moving, juddering up and down.

She felt sick.

In fact, now she thought about it, she was going to *be* sick.

'Don't!' Georgie snapped. 'I can tell you're about to, and I haven't a basin or anything. And the windows are screwed shut. So just don't!'

Lily swallowed painfully, and opened one eye, just a very careful slit. It felt as though she had to tear her lids apart.

'What happened?' she whispered. 'Where are we?'

'In a carriage, on the way to Fell Hall.' Georgie's eyes were so wide with fear that they seemed to have stretched. She gave a high, unnatural laugh. 'So we shan't need a railway almanac after all.'

Lily nodded, and then moaned as the pale green tendrils wrapped all round her again. It was as if an essence of the Dysart sisters had been poured into her skull. She vaguely remembered now. 'A spell...' she murmured.

'Yes. Louis was right – the Queen's Men do use magic. It was in a bottle. He threw it at us, don't you remember?'

'Almost. Why am I so much worse than you?'

Georgie sighed. 'You fought more. And you had more magic to overcome in the first place. You've been unconscious for over a day, I think. I was too, for a while. The spell seemed to hit you first, as though it knew the stronger one to go for. But once you fainted, it felt like someone strangling me. It was morning, when I woke up, and we've been travelling all through the day. We've only stopped to change horses, three times. And now it's getting dark again.'

'They didn't take Louis too?' Lily blinked wearily. 'I saw him in the passageway.'

'Penelope and Cora told the officer that Louis had

no magic – it was only us. But even then he was fighting, and saying it wasn't fair, we hadn't done anything. I tried to tell him that it was – it was all right.' Her voice wobbled as though she didn't really think it was. 'Aunt Clara hustled him away. She said that we must have bewitched him.'

Lily suddenly hauled herself upright, and then moaned, pressing her hand against her mouth.

'Sit still!' Georgie hissed. 'I can't travel all the way to Derbyshire in a coach you've been sick in. And there's no point calling for the coachman to stop, or anything like that – they won't. I tried, when you wouldn't wake up.' She put an arm around Lily, gingerly. 'I was worried about you – I wasn't sure you'd ever wake up.' She sighed. 'I'd have been a lot nicer when you did, if it wasn't for you almost being sick.'

'Henrietta!' Lily gasped, when she finally judged it was safe to move her hand. 'What happened to Henrietta?'

Georgie's eyes filled with tears. 'I don't know. The spell took her too. I'm sorry, Lily.'

'We left her behind?' Lily whispered, as Georgie's arms went round her.

'We couldn't do anything else. We were unconscious. And we can't do anything now, Lily, before you try. The coach is all muffled up, like Aunt Clara tried to do with the house. I can hardly even feel my magic.'

'But what will they do with her?' Lily rubbed her cheek against Georgie's pale pink sleeve, just as Henrietta used to. It was very soft, but it didn't make her feel any better. Now that Georgie had told her, she could feel the enchantments round the coach. Her magic was squashed down inside her, and it was hard to breathe. 'Aunt Clara doesn't like dogs. What if they drown her, Georgie?'

'They wouldn't…' But Georgie didn't sound very sure. 'Henrietta's too clever. And she isn't real, Lily, she's painted. She probably only drowns in turpentine. If they try to drown her in the river, she'd just swim away, and adopt some other poor soul to be her slave.'

Lily sniffed. It might well be true, though she could tell that Georgie was just saying anything she could to cheer her up.

'But what shall we do without her?' she asked miserably, and Georgie sighed.

'I don't know. I don't know anything. This was what we wanted, Lily, but I thought we'd be outside Fell Hall. Not shut in with the others. It's all gone wrong. I'm scared.'

Lily hid her face in Georgie's grubby sleeve. 'Me too.'

'We're slowing down.' Lily looked out of the window, but it was still too dark to see much, except for a glimmer of lamps.

'Perhaps to change horses?' Georgie suggested. 'We've been travelling all night.'

'Someone's by the door,' Lily whispered. She could hear scuffling, and then someone clearing their throat.

'I'm about to open this door, missies, and I warn you now, I'm armed. With a pistol, and with more of what you got the last time.'

'That spell…' Lily's eyes widened, and both girls shrank back against the dirty seat cushions.

The carriage door clattered open slowly, and the red-faced man glared in at them. The coachman was behind him holding up a lantern, and looking nervous.

'Good. Good. You're being sensible.' The red-faced man lowered the hand that held the small blue glass bottle a little. 'You may get out – to use the necessaries. But I'll be outside the door, you hear me? You go one at a time, and I'll be holding on to the other one, understand?'

The girls nodded, and hurried out of the carriage, allowing the man to march them to the small inn, and an unpleasant-smelling privy.

'Remember I have your sister,' he muttered to Georgie, as she bolted the door.

'And you just behave, miss,' he added to Lily. She nodded faintly. Walking had brought back her wish to be sick, and she had no intention of trying to escape. She was fairly sure she couldn't, even if he had obligingly lain down and died.

Eventually Georgie came out, looking as pale as Lily. 'It's disgusting,' she complained to their guard, who only shrugged.

'You're not living in a smart town house now, miss,' he pointed out, pushing Lily through the door.

The privy smelled unbelievably bad, and Lily was sick – but at least she felt slightly better afterwards. For a few seconds, until the general misery of their situation overcame her again.

'That really was a most uncouth noise,' someone whispered, from behind the old towel that Lily had refused to touch. She had splashed the water from the jug on her face and hands, and dried it on her skirt. The towel looked as though it were breeding things. And now it was talking. Lily leaned against the dirty whitewash of the wall and sighed. The spell hadn't worn off yet then. She was hallucinating.

'Aren't you going to talk to me?' A little black face peered out from behind the greyish folds of the towel, and Lily sobbed.

'Go away! It isn't fair!'

'I'm real, you idiot,' Henrietta snapped. 'Their spell wasn't that good. Now, you have to smuggle me into that carriage; I can't ride on the footplate any longer. I'm not a carriage dog, and I've already fallen off twice.'

Lily gaped at her for a second, and then the guard beat on the door, shouting at her to hurry, and she gave up wondering how Henrietta had managed it, and tore off the second layer of her petticoat, bundling Henrietta into it. Then she unlatched the door. 'I'm sorry to take so long,' she whispered. 'I do feel so dreadfully sick, and there isn't a bowl or anything in the coach. I've torn out my petticoat, you see. So if I'm sick again, at least I've got *something*.'

Georgie was staring at her suspiciously, but the guard simply nodded. Lily suspected it was his job to clean the carriage, and made herself wobble all the way back, clutching the petticoat to her mouth in a convincing manner.

She made herself wait until the coach was moving again before she put it down, and let Henrietta out.

'You found her!' Georgie squealed, and then put her hand over her mouth. They didn't know how much the guard and the coachman could hear from the box. But the coach rumbled on.

'She did not, I found *her*,' Henrietta said proudly. She shook her ears. 'Louis helped,' she admitted.

'Louis? Really?' Lily looked surprised. 'What happened?'

'It took a while for them to put you into the carriage

– I think they had to send for this one, it must have some kind of protection worked into it. Anyway, there was a little time, and they were so worried that you might wake up, no one was really watching me.' Henrietta licked Lily's cheek apologetically. 'I didn't want to leave you, but after what Louis had said about Fell Hall, I was sure that they were going to take you there. I needed to make sure I wasn't left behind.'

Lily pulled her closer, wrapping the torn petticoat around the little dog more tightly. No one was going to take her away. 'You're so clever,' she muttered thankfully.

Henrietta dipped her head gravely – although it was hard for her to look serious, swathed in lacy flounces as she was. 'Yes. But even I couldn't have done it without Louis. Probably.'

Lily frowned. 'Last I saw of him, Aunt Clara was dragging him away somewhere.'

Henrietta sniffed in disgust. '*She* lost no time disowning you both. So shocked that she had been housing magic under her roof. Horrified that the little minxes might have corrupted her dear son. And so on and so on. She sent Louis upstairs, she didn't want the officer looking too closely at him, in case he took it into his head to examine the rest of the family for magic. But Louis crept back down – he saw me coming out of the

113

study. He was sure they'd send you to Fell Hall too. He smuggled me out of the kitchens under his jacket – which is more dignified than a petticoat, Lily, but I suppose you were doing your best with what you had at hand.' She gave her another forgiving lick. 'We were just in time to see this carriage draw up. And so I hid underneath it, and then jumped on to the footplate as you set off. Thank goodness the streets were too busy for them to drive fast. But then once we got on to the road out of London, and they picked up speed…' She shuddered. 'The first time I fell off I had to run after the coach for at least half a mile. Luckily, there was a farm cart, I had a chance to catch up.' She sounded matter of fact, but Lily could see that one of her claws was half torn out of its pad, and there were traces of dried foam around her muzzle. The little pug had run after them until her paws bled.

'I can't do any spells in here,' Lily murmured miserably, stroking the injured paw. 'I can't heal it.'

Georgie passed her a fine lace-edged handkerchief – which she hadn't needed to, as Lily could have used a torn-off frill from the petticoat to bind up the bleeding pad. But she knew why Georgie had done it. Her sister hadn't always got on with Henrietta. It was a gesture.

Henrietta dabbed Georgie's hand with her nose gratefully. 'You're a good girl.'

Then she yelped and snapped, as Lily tried to wrap up her paw. 'Let me do it! Ugh.' She tugged at the handkerchief with her teeth. 'That will do, for the moment.' She sighed. 'I don't suppose either of you managed to be imprisoned with any food?'

The carriage stopped twice more to change horses, but the girls were not allowed out again. Georgie had dozed fitfully, slumped in the corner of the carriage, but Lily hadn't felt like sleeping. The spell that had knocked her out had left her weary, but too scared to rest. She had never felt magic like it. It had been so strong.

'What sort of magic was that?' she asked Henrietta.

The pug sniffed. 'I don't know. It affected me too. I'm not a magician, of course, but I suppose you used a spell to bring me out of that painting. So a spell designed to work against other magic caught me as well. I had to have a little rest under your uncle's desk.'

Lily laughed. Far from just needing a rest, the spell had made her feel as though she'd died, but was somehow still there to see what was happening afterwards. Then, as she struggled and tore at the suffocating magic, it had taken her over completely – until she'd woken up. Even now she felt as though her magic had gone away, somewhere just out of reach. She couldn't tell if that was because of the original spell, or if it was just the dampening effect of whatever spells were on the carriage. Hopefully, once they got out, Lily would be able to get hold of her magic again. She missed it so much it hurt.

At least she had magic, though. She had some hope of fighting back. What had happened to Peter, when these same people had taken him? She bit her lip. There would have been no point in hurting him. So why would they? He would be at Fell Hall, safe. They just had to get him out again.

And themselves.

'It's very strange, this countryside,' Lily muttered. She supposed she didn't really know enough to say that sort of thing, her whole experience being one small island, and a train journey to London, but the Derbyshire hills felt completely unfamiliar. Peering at them from the small window of the coach, in the dawn light, Lily was almost sure they were the great velvet backs of some sleeping animals. Perhaps an enormous sleeping dragon, undulating across the landscape. The road wove between the crags, and here and there piles of rocks overhung them, teetering, just not quite enough to see.

'Do you think that's it?' Henrietta asked curiously. Lily was holding her up against the window, and she had the better view – Lily suspected that for the next few days, anything she asked Henrietta for would be greeted with a downturned muzzle, and a helpless wave of bandaged paw. The next few days... She shivered. Who knew what would happen, when they reached Fell Hall?

She could see it now too. A pale house, surrounded by trees. It was very beautiful, from the swift glimpse she got as the road curled round another hill, but it didn't look welcoming. The white stone marked the green landscape like a scar.

The carriage jolted as they moved from the stone road to a gravelled drive, shaded by enormous trees, and Georgie woke up with a start.

'Are we there?' she gasped.

Lily nodded. 'Almost.'

Henrietta wriggled down from her lap, and nosed about the floor of the carriage, limping mournfully. 'Aha. I thought so. There's a foot-warmer – I'll hide behind it when we stop, and then I can sneak out when no one's looking.'

'Are you sure?' Lily asked anxiously, imagining Henrietta transported all the way back to London.

'Of course I'm not sure!' Henrietta growled. 'How can I be? But have you got a better idea? I don't think that wrapping me up in a petticoat is going to work now, is it?'

Lily shook her head. 'I suppose not. Just...well, make

sure you find us,' she added, shivering as the great stone house appeared at the end of the drive.

'I promise I will,' Henrietta murmured, as she disappeared under the seat, and the carriage rolled to a stop.

Lily shrank away from the window as a dark figure blocked out the light, and the door handle rattled. She hated herself for being so feeble, but the idea of another dose of the spell was terrifying.

The red-faced guard opened the door, and muttered, 'Come on out, then. Don't try anything.'

'I'm quite sure they won't,' a sweet voice murmured. 'They look such well-behaved girls.'

Lily swallowed, and reached out for Georgie's hand, and they stumbled down the steps.

A young woman was standing there smiling at them, in such a pleasant, friendly way that Lily automatically smiled back. Then she noticed that the red-faced guard had turned a greyish-pink, and wondered if someone scarier was standing behind the pretty, brown-haired woman. There wasn't. It was her he was so frightened of.

'Good morning, girls. Your names?'

'Lily Powers. And my sister, Georgiana,' Lily murmured. She even bobbed a little curtsey, and the woman nodded approvingly.

'Very good. I am Miss Merganser. I am the warden of Fell Hall.'

It sounded more like a prison every moment, Lily thought, as they followed Miss Merganser up the steps into the house.

From close to, it was a greyish honey colour, not the stark white it had seemed against the trees. The same deadening spell from the carriage was wreathed all round it, but Lily was sure that she could sense something else underneath. It wasn't like Aunt Clara's house at all – there she'd felt stifled and wrong, all the time. But here there seemed to be a longing for magic. Perhaps Fell Hall had known magic before?

Or perhaps it was the other children, Lily thought suddenly, as she saw a tiny, thin girl in a grey pinafore hurry across the hall in front of them. She caught sight of Miss Merganser, and flattened herself against the wall, with her eyes downcast. Her lips were moving, Lily noticed, as they passed her. She was silently repeating something to herself, over and over again. Like a spell – although surely not, here.

Lily had taught herself to lip-read so she could understand Peter, so it was easy enough for her to see what the little girl was saying.

Please, please, please, please, please…

Miss Merganser led them into a pretty room, with

flowered silk curtains, and ornaments across the mantelpiece. It reminded Lily of the old rose drawing room at Merrythought, that same pleasant faded look. Except at Merrythought there had been paintings – family portraits, mostly. Here the walls were bare – but there were patches of darker, pinker silk, where there had been pictures once. The family had been removed.

Miss Merganser sat down in a pale pink armchair, her hands folded neatly in her lap, and gazed at them, still calmly smiling.

'Powers…' she murmured. 'Strangely appropriate. Do you understand why you are here?'

There was very little point denying their magic now, after the way Lily had fought. They nodded.

'Mr Berryford tells me that you, in particular, are quite the adept.' Miss Merganser laughed delicately at Lily. Then the smile disappeared. 'We do not have magic here.'

'There's a spell on the house,' Lily muttered stubbornly. They were just as bad as Aunt Clara, pretending that they had no use for magic – except when they needed it.

'Certain spells are still authorised. For protection. And control.' Miss Merganser eyed Lily thoughtfully, and opened the pretty embroidered bag that was hanging at her waist, bringing out a tiny blue glass bottle like the guard's. She fingered it lovingly. 'All the staff have these. And others, should we need them. But no spells are cast at Fell Hall, Lily. All the magic in this house is dead.'

Lily blinked. Fell Hall! She had suddenly remembered where she'd heard the name. The Fells had been one of the greatest magical families. The great last battle of the Talish War had been fought from here, by magic – how could she have forgotten? After the Decree, the house must have been seized by the Crown, and turned into the reform school. It was a cruel way to show how far the magical families had fallen.

'Only these bottled spells are used here – but don't make the mistake of thinking that they're not as strong as fresh ones.' Miss Merganser put her head on one side, like a little smiling bird. 'Or perhaps you won't. You felt our spells, didn't you? Mr Berryford said he had to use a remarkably strong dose on you, Lily dear. The sooner you understand that magic is wrong, the better you will find your time at Fell Hall. Perhaps, eventually, when you're older and wiser, you'll be able to leave.'

Lily swallowed. Perhaps... What did that mean? She had a horrible sense of the white stone walls closing in around her.

SEVEN

Miss Merganser delivered them to a classroom, which Lily was sure had once been the house's library. It was lined with shelves, but they were almost all empty. Perhaps the books had been burned, Lily thought with a shiver. The shelf nearest to the large desk at the front held a few tattered atlases, and something that looked very like Aunt Clara's embroidery book, but that was all.

A foxy-faced young man with a large reddish moustache was marching up and down at the front of the room, waving at the blackboard, on which was drawn a squiggly sort of map. 'Treachery! Defection to Talis, you see? Typical of magicians.' He was practically spitting with disgust. He glared at the front row of children. The littlest ones, who were sitting on a bench at the front, had clearly been trying not to fall asleep. Several of them had been hastily woken by their neighbours, or the older ones sitting in desks behind them, when Miss Merganser came in. Now they were all quite awake, their eyes flicking between the schoolmaster and the warden, as though they didn't know which one it was safer to offend.

Lily scanned the rows of weary-looking boys for Peter, but she couldn't see him. Where was he? Were there more boys elsewhere?

'This is what we have to weed out of you! Stand *up*!' the foxy man roared, finally noticing Miss Merganser and the girls.

One of the smallest children fell over instead, sprawling at Miss Merganser's feet. She looked up with a frightened gasp, and curled herself into a ball, clearly expecting to be struck down with something awful.

Lily picked her up. 'Had your feet gone to sleep?' she asked sympathetically. The same thing had happened to her, when she'd been curled up reading.

She could hear the indrawn breath from the rest of the class, and as the little girl scuttled back into her place, Lily glanced up at them, and then at Miss Merganser, who was still smiling.

'How very kind, Lily. But we do not encourage

talking during lessons. You will soon come to see how we do things, I'm sure. Mr Fanshawe, these are Lily and Georgiana Powers. Go and sit down over there, girls.' She drew the master aside, speaking to him in a low voice. She gestured to the bag at her waist, Lily noticed, more than once. Clearly she was telling him to beware.

Lily squeezed on to the bench seat of a long wooden desk, with Georgie next to her, and looked along the row of children. It was separated, girls on one side, and boys on the other. The rows of desks extended back all the way along the room, so that about forty children were squashed in.

Lily glanced around curiously under her eyelashes. She had so often wished she could go to school, but this wasn't quite what she had imagined.

A heavy bell clanged, and the children looked up hopefully, but didn't dare move, until Mr Fanshawe waved at them vaguely. Then they hurried out, seemingly desperate to get away from Miss Merganser.

'Us too, do you think?' Lily whispered to Georgie, who shrugged. The girl next to them grabbed Lily's hand, and pulled her after the others, hustling them all out of the door, along a passageway, and out to the terrace, which led on to tangled, overgrown gardens.

The girl, who had long gingery plaits, hurried them into a thicket of bushes, and gave an enormous deep gasp – as though she'd been holding her breath ever since they were back in the library. Several of the other girls from the class were squashed together on to an old stone bench, and they stared curiously at Lily and Georgie.

'Should we ask them about Peter?' Lily breathed into Georgie's ear. 'Or about the prison? If any of them know where it is?'

Georgie shook her head. 'Not yet. We don't want people to know we're from Merrythought too. If Mama's plot has been discovered, they might think we're involved. We've no idea what Aunt Clara told the Queen's Men. We have to be careful – we should wait.'

Lily nodded, eyeing the girls cautiously.

'Thank you for picking up Lottie,' the ginger-haired one told her gratefully. 'I'm Elizabeth.'

Lily looked at her curiously, and remembered that the little child who'd fallen over had gingery hair too. 'Is she your sister? Isn't she too young to be showing any magic?'

Elizabeth shook her head. 'That doesn't matter. Our grandfather was a magician, and once I started showing signs they took both of us away. Lottie might never have any magic, but it doesn't matter.'

'What sort of magic do you do?' Lily asked interestedly.

'I don't!' the other girl sounded horrified. 'I don't do *any*! I've almost completely lost the taint. I just need to work a little harder, and then they'll let me go home. Once I'm properly clean.'

'Oh…' Lily nodded. She wanted to argue, she hated the words the girl was using – magic wasn't *dirty* – but she didn't think it would be any use. 'How long have you been here?'

'A year…' Elizabeth's eyes reddened. 'I wish I could go home. Lottie's almost forgotten what our parents look like. They sent us a photograph, soon after we came here, but we haven't had any letters for ages now.'

'Don't families visit?' Lily asked. She didn't actually want Mama to visit, of course, or even Aunt Clara. But perhaps Daniel might come, if they wrote to him.

'Of course not,' Elizabeth muttered. 'How could they? We're dangerous.'

The other girls glared at Lily, as though they thought she was trying to upset them on purpose. 'Don't you know anything?' a small dark girl with curls asked disgustedly.

Lily's cheeks went pink, but she didn't snap. 'Not much. Our family lived on an island. We didn't see many other people. We don't know a lot about magic – the rules about it, I mean.' She had a sense that explaining Merrythought, and the plot, any more than this would be dangerous. By rights these girls should be in favour of breaking out of the school and restoring magic – it wouldn't even have surprised her if they thought assassinating the queen was a pretty good idea. But instead they all seemed to think they were in exactly the right place. It was as though they hated magic, far more than anyone else she'd met. No one had been this disgusted by it at the theatre.

'Doesn't anyone ever try to – er – get out?' she wondered. 'To go and see their parents, or anything like that?'

The little dark-haired one snorted. 'Of course not! Miss Merganser knows who all our families are. What do you think would happen to them if we ran away because we missed home?'

'Oh.' Put that way, it was rather obvious.

'It isn't worth getting into trouble trying to escape. It won't take you long to lose your magic, if you really try,' one of the other girls told Lily encouragingly.

'What happens if we *don't* lose our magic?' Georgie asked huskily.

The girls shrugged, and looked at each other twitchily. 'You stay…'

'There weren't any older children in that class, though. Hardly anyone as old as me even,' Georgie pointed out.

'It isn't good to fight the spells,' Elizabeth said slowly. 'It wears people out. And all magicians die young anyway,' she added matter-of-factly.

'No, they don't.' Lily stared at her. 'Our mother and father are still alive.'

'They really do.' The others nodded earnestly at Lily, and she could see that they believed it was true.

'They won't listen,' Georgie whispered in her ear. 'They must have been told it all their lives; magic's wrong, and magicians come to a bad end.'

Lily nodded. The other girls were looking at her and Georgie as though they were truly strange. 'Does everyone here feel that way about their magic? You all want it gone?' she asked cautiously. 'No one misses it? Even a little?'

They were staring at her distrustfully. At last, one pale, mouselike girl muttered. 'You can't say things like that. We'll all get into trouble if you say things like that.' And they all got up, and hurried away through the overgrown shrubbery, casting suspicious glances back at Lily and Georgie.

Lily slumped down on the bench, her head hanging. 'I thought at least now we might be with some people who understand about magic. Those girls aren't anything like us.'

'I know.' Georgie scowled, and then she gave a little

snort of laughter and sat down by Lily. 'Even I thought they were feeble.'

Lily went pink. 'You're not feeble.'

'You and Henrietta spend your whole time complaining about how feeble I am,' Georgie pointed out. She sounded almost cheerful, and Lily glared at her.

'What are you so happy for? We're stuck here!' she hissed.

'I know. It's what we've been dreading all this time – we've been found out. I can stop worrying that we're *going* to be found out now, don't you see?'

'It makes a certain sense,' a growly little voice put in from under the bench. 'We're going to have to escape though – you can start worrying about that instead. Don't draw attention to me, Lily, you idiot girl!' Henrietta snapped, as Lily jumped off the bench and came to hug her. 'What do you think would happen to a talking dog here? Any one of those girls would have turned me in for a biscuit. I may have to hide out in the gardens for most of the time – which means we really do have to escape, and soon. I am strictly an indoor creature.' She glanced resentfully at the shrubbery and shuddered.

The bell clanged dolefully again, and the girls looked back at the house.

'I suppose that means we have to go in,' Georgie sighed.

'Be sensible and try to fit in,' Henrietta told them, peeping round Lily's feet. 'I shall go exploring. If I can get into the house safely I will, so for goodness' sake be discreet if you see me. No, "Hello, Henrietta," mmm?'

'I won't,' Lily promised. 'It's a lovely house,' she said suddenly, and then stopped, surprised. She hadn't realised quite how much she liked it. 'There's something special about it,' she added thoughtfully. 'I just haven't quite worked out what it is yet.'

'We'd better run, look, they're all going back into the house,' Georgie tugged her arm, pointing at the stream of children hurrying across the terrace.

Elizabeth, the red-haired girl, saw them coming, and waited reluctantly by the doors, as though she'd been told to watch over them. 'Come on. We have to go down to the kitchens now for our cookery lesson.' She eyed them nervously. 'Just don't say anything else stupid, will you?' She glanced around carefully. 'Miss Merganser will be watching us all extra-carefully. She always does when new ones arrive, and we've needlework this afternoon.'

Lily wasn't entirely sure what this meant, but Georgie asked, 'She teaches needlework?'

Elizabeth nodded. 'Yes. The boys are lucky, they do gardening instead.'

Lily frowned. Less chance to speak to Peter, or ask the other boys where he was.

'She almost always bluebottles someone,' Elizabeth went on, shivering a little.

Lily giggled, and Elizabeth looked at her, shocked. 'It isn't funny!'

'Bluebottles! Yes, it is. Those great big flies, you know?'

'You've never seen her do it,' Elizabeth muttered. 'You wouldn't laugh.'

'They did it to us to get us here,' Lily told her soberly. 'I'm only laughing because I'm scared.'

Elizabeth nodded, as if this was an answer she understood. 'There are other things too,' she added. But then she glanced over her shoulder and closed her mouth quickly, as though she couldn't say anything else.

Lily and Georgie stared at her anxiously, and Lily wondered if it was the spells on the house that had silenced her. Or if she was just too frightened to speak.

'I can't sew,' Lily added at last, to break the eerie silence. 'Georgie can, but I'm terrible at it.'

Elizabeth sighed. 'Well – perhaps as it's your first day here...' she began, not very hopefully, but then she trailed off. 'Anyway. Kitchens.'

She hurried them in and out of wood-panelled passages, and through doorways where they half-fell down odd deep steps, where one part of the house seemed to have been joined on to another, as if they'd been clumsily stuck together. Lily had a sense that the house was very, very old. Much older than Merrythought. It was comforting. Fell Hall had been here a long time, and this was only a small part of its history. She could feel the difference between the house, and the sticky layer of spell laid on top of it. Under the spell was more magic, she was sure. Proper, lovely magic, that liked her. She wanted to tear apart the muffling spell with her nails.

'Do we get to explore?' she panted hopefully, as they raced after Elizabeth. Perhaps they could find Peter themselves. He had to be somewhere.

Elizabeth looked back, shrugging. 'I suppose, if you want. There's time after lessons. There isn't anything very exciting though. Just lots of empty old rooms.'

'Are there...?' Lily trailed off, not quite sure how to ask. 'Are there any other children? You know, kept anywhere else?'

Elizabeth shook her head, but her eyes had widened. 'I don't know what you mean,' she muttered, and hurried on ahead of them, fast, as though she wanted to get away.

Lily shrugged helplessly at Georgie. What could they do, if everyone was too scared to speak?

The kitchens were dark and burrow-like, but they smelled nice, and the kitchen staff weren't as frightening as Miss Merganser, or as shouty as Mr Fanshawe. One of the kitchen maids muttered something about magic being unnatural, especially if one tried to cook with it, but it sounded as though she'd been told to say it at every lesson, and she was getting it over in between rolling out the pastry. No one paid very much attention.

The rather lumpen, misshaped pasties they made were served up for lunch. After the way the girls had backed off from them in the garden, Lily wasn't too surprised that no one seemed very eager to sit close to her and Georgie. They were squashed up at the end of a table, next to Mary, the thin girl they'd first seen in the entrance hall, and a few seats away from Elizabeth, and her little group.

'Where did you come from?' Lottie, Elizabeth's little sister, asked them, stabbing uselessly at her pasty. Georgie cut it up for her, and the little girl nibbled pastry like a squirrel.

'A house on an island first,' Georgie explained to her. 'And then we lived with our aunt in London.'

'Were you hiding your magic?' Mary whispered curiously. 'You're very old, for it only just to have shown.'

Georgie glanced at Lily uncertainly. Should they admit to this or not?

Lily shrugged. It was fairly obvious that they must have been.

'Yes...' Georgie said slowly. 'Our family didn't

submit to the Decree. Our mother taught me magic.'

Lottie's eyes widened, so that she looked even more squirrel-like, all eyes and gingery hair, nibbling away. 'Can you do real spells?' she whispered.

'Not here,' Lily said hurriedly. It wasn't quite true. She was sure she could, if she tried hard enough. Georgie could too, but if she used all the power she would need to fight the enchantment around the house, it was sure to summon up the spells that Mama had set inside her. Those spells were quite capable of disappearing a small squirrel-child, and who knew what else.

'Oh.' Lottie nodded sadly. 'No one can.'

Perhaps she was too young to have understood all the evilness of magic, Lily thought. She certainly didn't seem as horrified as the others had been. Lily glanced around, and whispered, 'Perhaps you will, one day.'

Lottie laughed delightedly, and Lily saw Elizabeth giving her a suspicious glare a little further up the table.

'I wish I came from an island,' Lottie said chattily, shedding pastry crumbs everywhere. 'Me and Elizabeth used to live in Suffolk, until she made our front door fall down. Our mother forgot her key, you see, and we were locked out. Elizabeth was frightened, and the door hinges just went.' Lottie glanced around secretively. 'Lots of people saw,' she whispered. 'Someone told. Our mother didn't want us to go, but the men said we had to, and we might hurt people if we stayed. But we're going back when we're better.'

'Oh dear…' Lily murmured, and Georgie looked sympathetic. The thin girl, Mary, shivered.

'Did something like that happen to you?' Lily asked her curiously. She knew it was nosy of her, but Mary had talked about Georgie's magic, so it seemed a fair swap. And if Mary was happy to talk, perhaps she could lead her on to the subject of prisons.

Mary shook her head slowly. 'My parents…' she muttered, with her eyes fixed on her plate. Lily noticed that a burning red flush had spread across the tops of her hollow cheeks. 'I was a baby.' Suddenly she pushed her plate away, and jumped up, racing out of the room, leaving Lily staring after her, guilt-stricken.

'Well done!' Elizabeth hissed at Lily, and even Lottie looked rather accusing.

'I didn't mean to upset her,' Lily protested. 'We were just talking. Why did she run away?'

'She's one of the stone children.' Elizabeth sighed at her, in a patient sort of way. 'We'll show you, afterwards. For now, why don't you just keep quiet?'

After the meal, Elizabeth beckoned to Lily and Georgie, and Lottie ran after them, slipping her hand into her sister's.

'Where are we going?' Lily asked, as Elizabeth led them out past the kitchens again, to a little side door.

'The wall. Come on.'

The wall had been built at the same time as the house, Lily guessed. It was the same honey-ish stone, but mortared together in massive blocks, and topped with spikes. The spikes looked shinily new.

Elizabeth led them along in the lee of the wall, wading through the thick, damp grass that flourished in the shade. 'Here,' she muttered at last.

Lily looked where she was pointing. There was a strange, rounded lip jutting out of the wall. It seemed newer than the wall itself, as though it had been added not all that long ago.

'Is it a fountain?' Georgie asked, stroking the edge of the stone. It was almost basin-shaped, Lily thought. Half a bowl. There had been a little niche set in the stone pavilion at Merrythought, which had been a fountain once, pouring water into a shell-like stone basin.

Elizabeth laughed shortly. 'No. It's a wheel.' She touched the stone edge gingerly, as though she didn't like it. Then she steeled herself, and gave the stone circle a shove, so that it creaked and ground, and juddered around like a millstone. Once she'd started it, it turned more easily, and spun full circle, revealing the matching half of the stone bowl on the other side.

'I don't understand,' Lily said, shaking her head. 'What's it for?'

'Children.'

Lily started as Mary slipped out of the bushes behind them, her grey pinafore streaked with green, as though she'd been curled up there a while.

'It's to put children in,' she repeated, watching Lily's face. 'Children people don't want. Magician children. Little witch babies.'

'You put the baby in the half of the circle that's outside the wall,' Elizabeth explained.

'Then you ring the bell, you see?' Lottie put in, pointing up to the black iron bell dangling above their heads.

'And someone comes and takes the baby in,' Lily said slowly. 'Are there a lot of the stone children?'

'Only me, and one of the boys, at the moment. I think it was commoner just after the Decree, when people were really scared. Seeing magicians everywhere.' Mary stroked the smooth stone.

'But you can't tell if a baby has magic, can you? It doesn't show till later, I thought.'

Georgie shrugged. 'I don't know. Maybe sometimes. Or perhaps if people were just frightened? If a baby had strange-coloured eyes, or something like that.' She managed not to look at Mary as she said it.

'Nothing magical's happened to me yet. So maybe I just looked wrong,' Mary said, in a flat little voice.

Lily wanted to say something comforting – something to cheer Mary up. But she really couldn't think of anything at all.

EIGHT

Lily had expected that a reform school would mean working all the time. She'd even had vague ideas of a giant treadmill hidden in the cellars, perhaps powering some strange furnaces. But from what the others told them, apart from lessons in the mornings, and needlework and suchlike after lunch, it seemed the children at Fell Hall were left to amuse themselves.

The girls had been given one of the parlours, where there were a few tattered books, and an assortment of old furniture that had been exiled from the smarter rooms. A similar room further down the passage housed the boys, but in the summer weather they stayed mostly in a hideout down by the lake, so Elizabeth told them.

Upstairs there were two long, chilly dormitories, with

rows of ugly metal beds. Lily stared down the girls' dormitory in horror. She had always had her own room at Merrythought, and at the theatre she'd only had to share with Georgie, and there had been plenty of other hidey-holes around the warren-like building. How could she ever be on her own here?

'I'm not sure how Fell Hall is supposed to be reforming us,' Lily murmured to Georgie as they got ready for bed on that first night. 'It can't just be lessons where Mr Fanshawe shouts about how awful magic is, can it?'

'The spells in the blue bottles, I suppose,' Georgie said sadly, holding up the skimpy white cotton nightgown she'd been given. Tomorrow they would have to wear the same white blouses and grey pinafore dresses as the other girls, and Georgie was missing the clothes from Aunt Clara's house already. 'And perhaps Miss Merganser's meant to terrify us into giving up magic. It would work on me.' She looked Lily up and down. 'That nightdress is horrible.'

'So is yours,' Lily pointed out.

Sarah, one of the few older girls, about the same age as Georgie, came in to the girls' dormitory carrying a huge tray, laden with thick white china mugs. A pleasant smell of chocolate floated across the room, and Lily's nose twitched.

'Cocoa!' Sarah yelled, and the girls hurried between the iron bedsteads to fetch their cups.

'You see?' Lily muttered, frowning. 'It isn't like a prison, at all. They're all lining up to get their cocoa! Cocoa, honestly.'

'Are you really complaining because Fell Hall is too nice?' Georgie asked her.

'Yes. I don't trust it.' Lily sat down on the lumpy bed, and folded her arms. 'I'm not having any. I'm full, anyway.' A lifetime of scratched and stolen meals at home meant that a whole dinner – even the solid, uninspiring food at Fell Hall – felt like a feast. The idea of a mug of cocoa on top actually made her feel queasy.

'Well, I'm having some.' Georgie had a taste for chocolate, from sharing violet creams with Maria and the ballet dancers in the theatre wardrobe. She went to fetch her cup, and came back with one for Lily too. 'I told Sarah you didn't want it, but she said Miss Ann – that's the pasty one who follows Miss Merganser around, isn't it? Anyway, Miss Ann would fling it at her, she said, if she didn't give them all out.'

Lily sighed, and glanced around. Most of the girls were still changing, or sitting drinking their cocoa. Only Lottie was looking at her. She put her finger to her lips, winked at Lottie, and poured the cocoa out of the window next to her bed.

Lottie giggled, and pattered over to whisper in Lily's ear. 'That's clever. I don't like it either, but I give mine to Elizabeth. She loves cocoa.'

'I don't suppose you know, Lottie, if there's anyone hidden at Fell Hall?' Lily whispered back hopefully. 'A boy, a little bit older than me? Do they keep people upstairs anywhere?'

Lottie shook her head. 'It's all empty upstairs, I think. But I've never been up there.'

Lily sighed. How could they all be so quiet, and obedient, and just not curious? Maybe it was only that they'd been here so long, she thought with a shiver, pulling her blanket up round her ears. She supposed you could get used to anything. But she wouldn't…

Lily lay in bed that night, listening to everyone breathing. She wondered where Henrietta was sleeping. At least it was a warm night. But she missed the solid, wheezing lump curled up in the small of her back.

The gentle sighing of the sleeping girls was maddening. Lily gave up trying to sleep, and sat up in bed, with the blankets wrapped around her knees. Why didn't anyone else seem to feel the way she did? She was desperate to escape Fell Hall, but all the others seemed so resigned to being there. Even grateful, almost, that they were safely tucked away!

She looked across at Georgie, with her long fair hair

spread across her pillow. She was smiling in her sleep – dreaming of sewing, probably. Miss Merganser had been graciously approving of Georgie's needlework – luckily, she hadn't had time to examine Lily's.

Lily scowled. What was Georgie looking so happy for? They needed to be finding Peter and making their escape plans, not sleeping. It wasn't as if their family would get into trouble if they ran away. Lily sniggered to herself at the thought of the red-faced guard turning up at Merrythought. He would probably come back as a beetle – or inside out, depending on how bad-tempered Mama was feeling. Then she shuddered, remembering that Merrythought had been raided, and Mama was gone. She could be anywhere.

Lily wondered if her mother could have fought off the bottled magics the red-faced guard had used. They must have something similar to restrain prisoners. Her father hadn't been able to resist them – unless he hadn't tried. He had sounded so *good* in the letter she had read, so very honest. Perhaps he had let them bind away his magic. Until now Lily had wanted to find him mostly for her sister's sake – her father was the only one they could think to ask to help them remove the buried spells. But now, cooped up in Fell Hall, and not even for a day, Lily knew she had to help him escape. She couldn't imagine what years of this must feel like. And what if

Penelope and Cora decided to make more trouble? There were all sorts of things they could accuse him of. Jonathan Dysart could probably have her father executed, if he wanted.

Whoever made those spell bottles must have been very strong. Lily folded her arms on her knees, thinking hard. How was it fair to punish her and Georgie and all these other children for using magic, when all the time Miss Merganser and the others were using it too, to keep them shut away?

Lily sighed, and stretched out her fingers, cautiously. There was a bubbling heat in her blood that made her almost sure her magic had come back. When she'd woken up from the spell that morning, she had thought for several awful moments that it was gone for ever. She couldn't imagine being without it. Especially after she'd spent a day being told that magic was dirty, and dead. It made her want to fling spells at people, cover them in glittering light, send them flying around the roof of this strange old house. Her fingers burned, and she sank her teeth into her bottom lip, hard. Not yet. She had to be careful.

Lily was almost sure someone sighed. She glanced suspiciously over at Lottie – had the little girl been awake and watching her? But Lottie was only a hump under her blankets. She must have imagined it.

What would happen if she did magic here? Were

there alarm spells? She couldn't sense them. But then, they wouldn't be much use if she could, would they?

All she could feel was the strange warmth, under the blocking spell. She reached for it, but there was that musty layer in between. Lily hissed with frustration. The spell wasn't actually as strong as the one Aunt Clara had created back in the London house. Their aunt's hatred of magic had repelled it like a waterproof cloak. This spell felt old. As though no one had paid much attention to it recently. Lily sniffed. If all the children at Fell Hall were as frightened as Elizabeth and her friends, it was no wonder. No one dared to do any magic here. The spell had nothing to work against. Why would anyone waste time renewing it?

'I wonder how far it goes up?' Lily muttered to herself. If no one used the attics and upper floors, perhaps the spell didn't cover them. She would go searching tomorrow, after she had found where they were keeping Peter. It still worried her that he wasn't with the other boys. What if they had sent him somewhere else after all? She couldn't think why he should be shut away, separated from all the others. Unless he'd been difficult, and it was one of the other things, the ones that Elizabeth couldn't bring herself to speak about. Lily shivered. Peter was very determined. And not easily scared.

What had he done?

She glanced over at Georgie, but her sister was so sound asleep, it would be a shame to wake her. She would tell her the idea about the spell in the morning, Lily thought sleepily, already half-dreaming.

She had to be dreaming. For how else would there be that strange, rustly voice in her head, whispering?

Soon, please! Soon!

NINE

Lily had to be shaken awake the next morning, the last shreds of her dream shimmering away as Georgie muttered in her ear. Scales, glittering in the sunlight – and so much magic.

'Lily!'

Lily sat up, scowling. 'I'm awake! Stop shouting at me!'

'You need to be more careful – you were talking in your sleep. About things you shouldn't have been.'

Lily sighed. 'How am I supposed to stop that? I can't help what I dream about!'

Georgie shrugged helplessly. 'You'll have to. Come on. We have to do something called drill before breakfast.'

Lily fought her way into her grey uniform pinafore, splashed her face quickly from the jug of water at the end of the room, and hurried after Georgie and the others to the terrace.

Further down the gardens, the boys were already lined up in rows, swinging what looked like the clubs the jugglers at the theatre had used.

'Are they doing tricks?' Lily whispered, surprised. 'Aren't they meant to throw them?'

'They're Indian clubs,' Lottie told her. 'It's an exercise. We aren't allowed them, which isn't fair, they look much more fun than drill.'

Lily was about to ask her what drill actually was, but Miss Merganser marched out to the front of the terrace, wearing a white blouse, and what Lily thought was a rather daring divided skirt.

'That's improper,' Georgie muttered, conveniently forgetting that they had worn much more improper costumes themselves. 'What does she think she looks like…'

Lily thought she looked quite sensible, but Miss Merganser was already glaring at them, so she didn't say anything.

'Arms!' Miss Merganser barked. 'Right arm. One!'

Resignedly, the three rows of girls raised their right arm straight out to the side to shoulder height.

Lily and Georgie quickly did likewise.

'Two!'

Everyone put their arms down again.

'Left arm. One!'

Lily glanced hopefully sideways as she lifted her arm – yes, she was doing it right.

It went on for ever – or so it seemed. Arms. Legs. At least five minutes of simply turning their heads from one side to the other. Miss Merganser shouted at her, because she didn't have her hands properly on her waist. Fingers were to face forward. The rest of the class eyed her pityingly.

'Do we have to do that every day?' Lily whispered to the girl in front of her, as they marched back into the house.

'Drill has been proven effective in occupying restless energies.' Miss Merganser seemed to have appeared from nowhere. 'Which you clearly have, Lily Powers. Your display was despicable. You had better miss breakfast. Go and stand outside the schoolroom.'

Lily sighed, and trudged away. She wasn't used to that much breakfast at home anyway, even though the food at Aunt Clara's had been a great deal more plentiful. She would manage.

She occupied the time trying to remember her dream, as she stared vaguely at the carved wooden staircase in front of her. She hadn't noticed as she'd been hurrying up and down those stairs – usually with someone shouting at her – but there were creatures carved into the banisters here and there. Strange snakes or lizards hiding in the leafy branches that made up the main pattern.

Glancing quickly down the passage to the dining room, Lily stepped away from the schoolroom door to stroke the little wooden beasts, tracing her fingers over the carvings. They were definitely lizards, not snakes; they had legs. But there were odd bumps on their backs too. She'd taken them for part of the spray of carved flowers that curled above the creatures, but now she was closer, and it was clear that they were meant to be growing out of the scaly backs.

'Wings,' she muttered, and smiled to herself. 'Dragons.' Had no one else ever noticed them? The portraits of the magicians had been taken down, and the magical books removed. She would have expected that these sly little beasts would have been cut out – or at least had their telltale wings removed.

As she thought it, she heard a sharp, tapping tread further down the corridor, and she shot back to her place outside the door so quickly that the carvings seemed to move. She could have sworn the wings fluttered in dismay, stretching out as though their owners wanted to check they were still there. Had they heard what she was thinking? But she couldn't look again to check. Miss Merganser was marching down the passage towards her, and even though Lily had never been to school, she knew enough to keep her head down, and look sorry.

'Well, I hope missing your breakfast has shown you the error of your ways,' the warden told her sweetly, and Lily shivered. Miss Merganser's voice had no spells in it to make it so unnerving. It was just her, which made it almost worse.

She nodded.

'Speak when you're spoken to!'

'Yes, Miss Merganser.' Lily glanced up, carefully not looking at the banisters, in case they twitched again.

'Very well. You may go and sit in your place, and wait for the others.' Her sharp-heeled boots pattered away, and Lily chanced another look at the carvings. But they were still now, even when she touched them. She wondered how old they were. The tops of the banisters were worn into smooth waves with what must be hundreds of years of hands stroking down them. If the staircase was part of the original house, Lily was fairly sure it had been built in the 1500s. There had been a particularly famous Fell, who had been granted the land by the king. She had read about him, hiding from the sea wind behind a gorse bush on the cliffs, back at Merrythought. It had started to rain, though, and Lily wasn't sure she had ever finished the book.

Her eyes widened as she remembered the illustrated heading of the chapter on the house of Fell. Richard Fell had been rumoured to own a dragon…

'I thought you were going to lie low!' A snarl sounded somewhere around Lily's ankles. 'We're not supposed to be drawing attention to ourselves, remember? What are you doing getting yourself into trouble?'

Lily's heart jumped inside her, half with fright and half with happiness, and she caught Henrietta up in her arms. 'You got inside!'

'Sshhh,' Henrietta said disapprovingly, but she did lick Lily's ears. 'Someone left those doors to the terrace open. Now you'd better hide me in this schoolroom she was talking about.'

Lily nodded. 'I will. I know a place, there's a window seat, and wooden shutters you can sit behind. But Henrietta, look at these.'

She held the little pug up to the banisters, and Henrietta frowned. 'Dragons. What of them?'

'The Fells are supposed to have had real ones, aren't they?'

Henrietta snorted. 'That's just a myth! No such thing.'

'These ones moved,' Lily muttered stubbornly. 'I saw them.'

'And that spell has addled your wits.' Henrietta nudged her with a cold nose. 'Hide me!'

Lily hurried into the schoolroom, tucked Henrietta at the back of the window seat, and sat down beside her. 'Where did you sleep last night?' she asked.

Henrietta assumed a mournful expression. 'In a shed...' she sighed. 'Arabel *never* made me sleep in a shed, Lily.'

'I know. I'm sorry,' Lily told her humbly.

'If it wasn't for the good of the family, I wouldn't be doing it.' Henrietta eyed her sternly. 'I shall expect to be very thoroughly thanked, when we eventually sort all this nonsense out. Maybe even a statue.' She shifted her paws, and tilted her head a little, and Lily could see that she was practising her statue pose.

'Henrietta, we've been shut up in a reform school. We've got nowhere finding Peter. Father's in prison, and everyone in the country either thinks magic is evil, or else they *are* magical, and they're plotting to overthrow the government, as far as I can see.' Lily drew her knees up and tucked them under her pinafore. 'I'm not saying you can't have a statue,' she added. 'I just think it might take a while...'

Henrietta sniffed. 'I can wait. But I shall hold you to

it, Lily, mind. Have you managed to do any spells here yet? Is your magic working?'

'I think it will, but there's a spell that's meant to stop us doing any,' Lily explained. 'It's old though, almost worn out. If we go exploring up to the top of the house, I think it'll be even thinner. I'll be able to get out of it.'

Henrietta nodded approvingly. 'Good. This afternoon, then. You'd better go and sit in your place, Lily, I can hear people coming.'

'Be good.' Lily eyed her anxiously. 'I don't think you'll like Mr Fanshawe; he's supposed to be teaching us how awful magic is. He might say things you don't agree with…'

'You do that all the time,' Henrietta told her, curling up in a smooth little ball. 'And I simply ignore you. Don't fuss, Lily. I can manage to keep myself quiet.'

Lily spent Mr Fanshawe's lesson trying to watch Henrietta's window without being too obvious about it, and flinching every time he said something that she knew the dog would disagree with. Henrietta did manage to control herself, but Lily noticed the shutters shaking a couple of times, particularly when Mr Fanshawe was talking about tainted families, and degenerate magicians.

She lingered in the classroom as the others hurried

outside. Georgie nudged her as the last of the girls raced out of the doorway. 'Was that Henrietta?'

'Did you see her?'

'No! I saw you! Twitching and jumping all the time. You really couldn't have looked any more suspicious. We have to be careful, Lily. I'm going to talk to Sarah.' Georgie sighed crossly, and stalked out of the room, leaving Lily gaping after her. She was sure she hadn't been that obvious. And why was Georgie so angry?

Henrietta nosed her way out from behind the shutter, and gazed at Lily, with glinting eyes. 'This place is working on her already.'

'It can't be. We've only been here a day and a bit! She knows how important it is that we find Peter, and then rescue Father and get those spells out of her.'

Henrietta stretched out her front paws luxuriously, and yawned. 'But you're forgetting, she's already weakened by the very spells you want her to get rid of. Your mother half-broke Georgie, setting them inside her. I've teased her unfairly, I think.' Henrietta glanced up wickedly. 'Not that I intend to stop, it's far too much fun.'

'We really need to get away,' Lily muttered.

'I shall go exploring upstairs.' Henrietta jumped down from the window seat. 'I shall wait for you, somewhere near the top of the third-floor stairs, after your lessons.' She nudged Lily's ankle affectionately. 'I'll smell you coming, don't worry.' She trotted to the door, peered round it, and shot away up the stairs.

Lily was shaking later, as she climbed the same staircase. Miss Merganser had got round to her needlework – or lack of it – and had ripped it apart in disgust. Her hand had been hovering over the pocket hanging from her waist where she kept the spell bottles, but in the end she had settled merely for shouting. But she had separated Lily from her sister, sending her to sit alone on the window seat where Henrietta had been hiding earlier. Georgie kept darting her furious glances, and Lily's eyes were so blurred with crying that she stabbed her fingers over and over, staining her sampler with a mixture of blood and tears.

'What have they done to you?' Henrietta growled, as Lily climbed the third staircase on trembling legs. The black pug circled around her feet worriedly, almost tripping Lily up.

'Nothing. Only shouted. I'd forgotten what it was like. No one ever shouted at us at the theatre, or only to say I had my dress sticking out of one of the hidden panels, or something like that. They weren't mean. And Mama was always meaner to Georgie than me.' Lily stumbled to the top of the steps, and sat down, wrapping her arms around her middle. 'It's stupid. It doesn't really matter.'

Henrietta leaned heavily against Lily's knee, and

whirled her tail. 'You need to do some magic. You're missing it, I can tell.' She tugged Lily's pinafore with her teeth. 'I think you're right about the dampening spell up here. I can't feel it at all, and the air seems fresher.' She looked up at Lily hopefully, but Lily was staring at the faded wallpaper, frowning.

'What's the matter?' Henrietta peered at it too.

'It moved! Like the banisters! I was just looking at the pattern – it's so faded, I was trying to see what it was – and it moved.'

'Looks like the family coat of arms to me,' Henrietta mused, jamming her nose up against the wall. 'That's very smart. A little showy, though, I think. It's hardly discreet, is it, slapping your family emblems all over the wallpaper?'

'So the Fell crest has a dragon?' Lily asked, tracing the faded, greyish figure coiling across the paper.'

'Yes. But they're still a myth.'

The worn old dragon seemed to wind itself around Lily's fingers, and someone laughed. Lily jumped back, pressing herself against the banisters.

Henrietta sneezed with surprise, and then stared suspiciously at the wallpaper.

'You heard that too, didn't you?' Lily whispered.

'Mmm,' Henrietta admitted. 'I might have done. No one followed you, did they?'

'No.' Lily ran her fingers gently across the paper again. 'Someone was already here.'

They hid themselves in one of the abandoned rooms, swathed in dustsheets. They had turned left at the top of the stairs. The right-hand passage seemed less dusty, as though some of the rooms might still be used. One of them, the first door down the passage, was locked, and Lily had started to call for Peter. Then she'd sighed at her own stupidity. He couldn't hear her. And if she tried to push a note under the door, Miss Merganser or one of the other staff might find it. She listened for a while, with her ear to the keyhole, but she couldn't hear anyone inside.

'He isn't there, Lily,' Henrietta told her impatiently. 'If he were, I would have smelled him. I know his scent.' She snuffled along the bottom of the door. 'I won't say there isn't someone in there, mind you. But it's not him.'

The left-hand passage looked safer, for a hidey-hole, as though they were less likely to be found.

Lily chose the room because of the overmantel, a fantastical white wooden explosion of swirls and scrolls. It matched the white dustsheets, and lent the whole room a curious dreamlike feel. Once she brushed away the dust furring over the curlicues, the carvings could have been snow, or even sugar.

'There's another one down here,' Henrietta muttered, almost reluctantly, nosing the marble mantelpiece surrounding the fire. 'Bigger than those others.'

Lily laughed when she saw him first – he looked like a dragon made of icing, something from a smart pastry-cook's shop. She wanted to lick her finger, when she'd dusted him, to see if it had come away sweet. 'He's beautiful,' she murmured, dusting him a little more with her grey dress – and the outstretched wings seemed to shimmer gratefully. 'Let's practise here.'

Lily wedged herself between the grate and the carving of the mantelpiece, and Henrietta climbed possessively into her lap.

'What shall I do?' Lily asked, rather helplessly. She didn't usually practise her magic – it just happened, when she needed it to. Now it seemed terribly important to choose the right spell. Something that would reawaken her damaged powers, and turn her back into the sort of person who could rescue friends. And fathers.

'Anything!' Henrietta snapped impatiently. 'You could rustle me up a nice ham sandwich. I tried to go ratting in the stables last night, and the rats were rather larger than I was.'

'Food's difficult,' Lily muttered. 'Especially when there isn't anything to start with. I'm sorry.' She stroked

Henrietta's ears. 'Miss Merganser was watching me all through lunch. I couldn't steal anything for you. Not even crumbs.'

'Mice taste most unpleasant, did you know that?' Henrietta told her gloomily. 'Especially raw.'

Someone chuckled behind them, and Henrietta turned round to glare at the marble mantel. 'It's very rude to break into a conversation when you haven't been properly introduced.'

A sense of apology seemed to hover in the air, and Lily stared hopefully at the stone dragon. It didn't move. But the apology died away, replaced with a glow of excitement that seemed to shimmer all through Lily too, warming her. It shifted the hard little stone of fright that had grown inside her, fright and worry and despair, and she smiled gratefully. Even Henrietta almost purred.

The marble dragon was shining, Lily realised, as she stroked it lovingly, the stone translucent, and almost soft.

'It's real,' she murmured.

'How can it be?' Henrietta sounded confused, and quite annoyed. 'It's a stone!'

'Not always. It's *been* real, Henrietta, I'm sure it has.' Lily blinked at her. 'And anyway, you were a painting!'

'Hmf. But that was a spell. You called me out. You're saying that this – stone – was real first?'

'I can't tell. It isn't just a carving, though. Can't you feel it?'

'I suppose so,' the pug muttered, and Lily suddenly realised that she was jealous.

'I chose you,' she whispered. 'You were my first spell, remember.'

'You're meant to be practising.' Henrietta jabbed her roughly with a cold nose.

Lily nodded. She reached out, and wrapped both hands around the strange soft stone of the dragon's body. Scales itched and glinted against her fingers, even though she couldn't see them, and the carving glowed brighter still. She could feel magic thrumming eagerly through the stone, like a warm little heart beating. And the eagerness! Something so wanted to break free.

But it couldn't, quite.

Lily's head swam, and Henrietta snarled. 'Lily, stop!'

Half-fainting, Lily's hands slid away from the stone, and she shook herself wearily.

Almost, something whispered gratefully. *Soon*!

TEN

'Was it really a dragon?' Lily whispered, when they were back in bed.

'I still say they're only a myth,' Henrietta muttered stubbornly. But she didn't sound quite as sure as before.

'It felt like the house.' Lily stared up at the dark ceiling of the dormitory. 'The spirit of the house. Perhaps it was just using that carved dragon to talk to us.'

'Are you planning to talk all night?' Henrietta growled, burrowing down further under the blankets. 'I'd be asleep already if I weren't so hungry.'

Lily smiled. She was tired too – wonderfully worn out, her magic stretched and limp. She had missed using it so much. She felt as if she was held together with damp string. She yawned suddenly, and tucked her knees round Henrietta. Whatever it was, dragon or not, she was almost certain it was an ally.

Lily woke the next morning almost eager to get to the schoolroom. The sooner they were done with lessons, the sooner she could hurry up to the third floor.

But everything changed at breakfast.

'There's a new boy, can you see him, Lily?' Lottie nudged her, as Lily stirred her porridge without enthusiasm. It was so horribly grey. A similar colour to her dress.

Lily looked up hopefully. She had begun to think that Peter wasn't at Fell Hall at all. But perhaps he had been hidden away somewhere. In one of the outbuildings. Or upstairs. Maybe even one of those rooms further down the right-hand side of the corridor? She felt a sudden stab of guilt. She shouldn't have listened to Elizabeth, she should have looked harder. She stared eagerly at the boys' benches, where Lottie was pointing.

Her spoon clattered against the bowl and sprayed greyish porridge over her greyish uniform.

Across the room, a thin, tanned boy with spiky brownish hair didn't look up.

He couldn't hear the sharp sound of metal hitting china, or Miss Ann's whining voice telling Lily to be more careful.

Peter just went on eating his porridge.

'He can't hear you. There's no point talking to him,' the curly-haired boy explained, staring at Lily and Georgie. 'What do you want to talk to him for anyway?' He sounded affronted, and he kept glancing shiftily at the door. Clearly he didn't want to get into trouble with Mr Fanshawe.

'We know he can't hear. Look, just go away, can't you? Then no one can tell you off for being with us.' Lily flapped at the boy dismissively, and he slunk into the next row of desks, scowling at her.

'Are you all right?' Lily demanded anxiously, making sure that Peter was looking straight at her. 'Where have you been? Were they keeping you somewhere else?' She shoved a piece of paper and a pencil in front of him, and stared at him expectantly. Last time she'd seen him, he'd been hiding under the jetty, at the bottom of the cliffs on Merrythought Island, on the night they'd run away. Peter had pushed their boat out into the water, and she'd begged him to come with them. But he hadn't dared. He'd been abandoned on the island years before, because his family hadn't wanted to raise a mute, or so everyone at the house decided.

Peter only stared at her blankly. His fingers twisted and reached towards the pencil, as though he half-remembered what it was for.

'They've been at him with that same spell they used on us, I think,' Lily muttered. 'It's like he's half-asleep.'

Heavy footsteps sounded outside the door, and Georgie tugged her arm. 'Lily, come on! We can't let them see we know him. The girls are already staring.'

Lily nodded, darting into her seat. No one at Fell Hall seemed to have worked out that Peter and the girls were all from Merrythought. She would rather it stayed that way. The less anyone knew about them the better.

Later that afternoon, Lily climbed the staircase again, sneaking around the corners, and darting from shadow to shadow. She had wanted to bring Peter and her sister with her, but Georgie was with Sarah again, strolling round the shrubbery with their heads together. And Peter didn't even seem to know who he was, let alone remember Lily. So she went back upstairs alone, desperate to talk to Henrietta.

The pug was sitting by the carved dragon, eyeing it worriedly.

'It doesn't feel the same,' she said, as soon as Lily slipped in the door.

Lily dropped down next to her, and stroked the dragon's stone back. Stone was all it was, this time. Disappointment flooded through her. 'Did we break it?' she asked miserably. Everything was going wrong.

Henrietta shook her head. 'I think it's gone somewhere.'

Even though the stone figure was still clearly sitting there, Lily knew what she meant. She ran her fingers down the stone scales. 'I found Peter.'

Henrietta blinked at her. 'Where is he then? Why didn't you bring him with you?'

'He wouldn't come.' Lily swallowed. 'I think they've broken him somehow. With the spells they use to fight our magic. And he didn't even have any powers! It's so stupid!'

Henrietta glared at the carving. 'We'll have to mend him, then. We should get this thing back. It must be magic, so it ought to be on our side, don't you think? It can't hurt, surely...' She licked the dragon's muzzle thoughtfully. 'It's *possible* that you set it free.'

'I was trying to,' Lily sounded doubtful. 'But I just got dizzy. Nothing happened.'

Henrietta shrugged. 'Maybe you woke it up enough that it set itself free.' She snorted. 'It's a dragon! Who knows what the rules are?'

'What if we never find it again?' Lily leaned back against the carving with a sigh. 'I was hoping it might help us escape, somehow.'

Henrietta huffed. 'If you did set it free, we'll probably never see it again. None of the myths about dragons ever said they were grateful. It's probably flapped off to the other side of the country.'

Lily shook her head. 'I don't think it would do that. It belonged here.' She sighed again, and heaved herself up from the floor. 'I suppose we should go back downstairs. I didn't tell Georgie about the dragon last night, I didn't know what to say. It would have sounded so strange. But I probably ought to now. Or she'll complain I'm keeping her in the dark.'

Henrietta lay down, resting her head on her paws and looking up at Lily mournfully. 'I'll stay here then. I'll try and creep into the dormitory later.'

Lily kissed the close-furred top of her head. 'I'll wait for you. I couldn't sleep without you, the first night.'

Henrietta ducked her head so as not to let Lily see her smugness. 'Well. I'll do my best then.'

Lily wandered miserably around the lower floors, searching for Georgie. She had to tell her what was happening. She hurried from the schoolroom, to the girls' common room, even to the outhouses, where no one with any sense would linger. Little knots of girls were everywhere, and they all seemed to be laughing. It made her feel desperately lonely. And cross. Why were they all so happy in this horrible place?

Lily found her eventually, huddled up next to Sarah in one of the old parlours. It had been a pretty room once, with soft sage-green silk on the walls, but now the colour had faded to a sickly grey. The delicate furniture that must have been there had gone, but there was still a cushion in the window seat, and Georgie and Sarah were sitting on it, sewing. They looked up as Lily came in, and glared at her. Both of them.

'What do you want?' Sarah snapped.

Lily blinked. She'd hardly spoken to Sarah, and certainly hadn't done anything to offend her. Why was the older girl being so unpleasant?

'Go away. We're busy. And your sister doesn't want to talk to you.'

'Georgie…' Lily started towards her, wanting her to tell Sarah to mind her own business. But after a couple of steps, she realised that Georgie wasn't even looking at her. She was staring at her needlework as though she'd never seen anything more fascinating.

'See?' Sarah sneered. 'She doesn't want to talk to you. Better for her if she doesn't, anyway. Anyone can see you're going to be trouble. Go on, run away and play.'

Lily did. She was ashamed afterwards. She should have yelled. Grabbed Georgie and dragged her away. But just then she couldn't think of anything to yell, except how much she hated Fell Hall. So she ran, slamming the door behind her, and hurried off down the dusty passage, refusing to cry again.

In the end she went to bed. There didn't seem to be anything better to do, and she was still tired after the huge effort of the spell the night before. She lay huddled under her blankets, worrying about Georgie. Her sister was taking the teaching at Fell Hall to heart. Georgie already hated her magic, the way it was tied up with Mama's cruel spells. She did everything she could to avoid using it. It wouldn't be hard to persuade her that magic itself was evil. That was bound to be exactly what Sarah had been telling her, Lily thought dismally. That, and how to pretend she didn't have a sister.

She was half woken by Sarah herself, complaining.

'She has to drink her cocoa!'

'She's asleep. Don't wake her up. Look, if you're going to get into trouble about it, I'll drink it for her.'

Lily wriggled in her sleep, wanting to wake up and tell Georgie not to, although she wasn't quite sure why. It seemed terribly important somehow. But she was weighted down with sleep, and the voices died away.

A little later – in her sleep, it seemed hardly any time at all – Lily began to dream, wonderful flashes of flight, soaring and dipping over the stone crags they had seen on their way.

Who are you?

They both thought it at the same time, and a deep, throaty chuckle made the bed shudder.

Are you sure you're not a Fell, little one?

No. I'm Lily, Lily Powers. From Merrythought.

I don't know that name. There's Fell blood in you, I'm sure. A distant cousin perhaps. Welcome, cousin.

Who are you? Lily asked again, hoping she knew.

Oh, you do know, cousin. But you have to believe in us enough to say.

Us? There are more of you?

There was a soft sigh, and Lily felt whatever it was – no, the dragon. She *did* believe. She felt the dragon slip a little further away.

There were...

Lily twitched, and huddled closer to the warm bulk down the side of the bed, holding it close and tight. It was warm but strangely smooth and hard – like one of the clay hot-water bottles they'd had at Merrythought. Just much, much bigger.

As she woke up enough to start wondering about it, suddenly it wasn't there any more. Lily sat up, confused. She had been lying on something. She knew she had. Blinking, she looked across at Georgie's bed, to ask her sister what was happening.

Georgie gasped. 'Lily, what have you done to your face?'

Lily shook her head. 'Nothing. What do you mean?'

Georgie crept over to her, and stroked her fingers

down Lily's cheek. 'It's as though you've pressed your face on to something. What have you been sleeping on?' She lowered her voice to a worried hiss. 'It can't be Henrietta. Besides, I can see her in a lump down the bottom of your bed. This looks like *scales*.'

Lily swallowed. The middle of the crowded dormitory wasn't the place to tell Georgie she might have dreamed a dragon into life. Besides, from the look on her sister's face, even if the dragon was actually there, and prepared to fly them out of Fell Hall on embroidered cushions at that very moment, Georgie wouldn't be going. Lily was pretty sure that she had been listening to Sarah dripping poison all day yesterday. *And she drank two cups of that cocoa last night*, a small voice in the back of her mind pointed out.

'Pull your hair over your face, for heaven's sake,' Georgie muttered.

Lily did as she was told, hurrying through her dressing. How was she going to stand that stupid drill, when all she wanted to do was talk to Peter? Their escape plan needed to happen now – before Georgie renounced her magic for ever. Lily ground her teeth fiercely as she tied her boots. If she had to drag Georgie over the wall by her hair, they were getting out.

She would just have to leave the dragons behind.

ELEVEN

Lily could see that Miss Merganser was watching her closely, just waiting for her to make a mistake – to swing her arm left instead of right, for instance, as though the world would end if she did.

Lily concentrated. She didn't have time to go and stand outside the schoolroom – although she would like to look at the wooden dragons again. Were all the pictures and carvings round the house one dragon? Or if she woke them up, would she be talking to a different creature?

Suddenly she snapped back to the drill class, just in time to change to raising her left foot to knee height – and not an inch higher, as that would be indelicate.

Miss Merganser looked quite disappointed, she thought.

Lily hung back as the others went into breakfast, waiting to catch Peter as the boys streamed across from their Indian club-waving. As she'd expected, he was following on behind – the other boys had no idea how to talk to him, and so they left him alone.

She'd hidden herself behind one of the doors, so that she could grab him as he went past. Luckily he was far enough after the other boys that no one would see them talking. As he came in from the garden, blinking in the gloom, she stepped out eagerly.

But he shrank back from her, a look of horrified surprise on his face.

'What's the matter?' Lily asked, feeling hurt. She put her hands on his shoulders, turning him to face her properly, so he could read her lips.

He pulled away from her sharply, leaving her staggering, and she stared at him.

'What is it?' she murmured helplessly.

Peter reached into his pocket, drawing out a small slate, which Mr Fanshawe must have given him. He scratched on to it with sharp, anxious strokes of the pencil.

Who are you?

'It's the cocoa.' Henrietta nodded gloomily. 'It can't be anything else. The spell on the house isn't strong enough to make him forget who you are.'

'Is it drugged?' Lily whispered. She couldn't do much more than whisper. She'd been crying so hard that her voice hurt, and her eyes were swollen. Somehow she had managed to last through lessons, and lunch, and even needlework, but the moment they had been dismissed, she had fled upstairs to find Henrietta, so they could grieve together for the friend who had disappeared. She had lost Peter and Georgie was almost gone. They were all alone now.

'Spelled.' Henrietta sniffed. 'I shall see if I can get a taste of it tonight. Some of them leave their cups on the floor – I've seen them do it when I've been hiding behind that locker of yours.'

'Don't!' Lily gasped.

'It won't work on me, stupid girl. Not if I only have a lick. But I might be able to tell what it is.'

Lily sighed, and pulled a dustsheet from an ancient-looking claw-footed armchair. She wrapped it around herself, and curled up in the chair, burying her face in the cushioned pink velvet. Crying had left her shivery and aching. Henrietta scrabbled her way on to the chair, and burrowed between Lily and the arm, where she promptly went to sleep. Worn out by crying, Lily soon followed her.

She woke some time later, confused by the strange light in the room as she half-opened her eyes. It was early evening, and the sky had been overcast all day. But now the room was bright. She sat up suddenly, her heart thudding. If someone had brought a lantern, then they had been discovered.

There was no lantern. Instead, seated in front of the fireplace, sitting up on its hindquarters rather like a dog, was an enormous, winged creature. The soft white light was coming from its silvery scales.

Lily swallowed. 'I told Henrietta you were real,' she found herself saying.

'I am not quite real yet…' the dragon told her thoughtfully. 'I shall be soon, though, I think.'

A muffled whine sounded from beside Lily, as Henrietta woke up, and saw who she was talking to.

'What a curious little creature.' The dragon lowered its muzzle – which was now about the size of a tea tray – to inspect Henrietta. 'Is it a dog?'

'Of course I'm a dog!' Henrietta snapped. The easiest way to distract her from anything was to insult her, as Lily well knew. 'What are you?'

'The oldest of the Fell Hall dragons.' The dragon settled back on to its haunches, still eyeing Henrietta in fascination. 'You do not look like a dog. I know dogs. You are too small.'

'Too small!'

Lily seized Henrietta by the collar before she flung herself at the dragon. He was a hundred times larger than she was, but Henrietta tended to lose all common sense when she was infuriated.

'She's a pug. They were bred in China.' Lily gazed thoughtfully at the dragon. 'Have you really never seen a dog like her?'

The dragon shook its enormous head. 'Wolfhounds, I know. Gazehounds. Mastiffs.'

'I'm not actually sure what a gazehound is,' Lily admitted. 'Have you been not real for a long while?'

The dragon looked uncomfortable for the first time. Its dark, glittering eyes shifted away from Lily, as it tried to think. 'It may be so,' it admitted finally. 'What year is this?'

'Eighteen ninety-one,' Lily told him, curiously.

The dragon's claws scraped across the floorboards convulsively, but there were no marks. It was still only half real. 'Three hundred years, then.'

'Why?' Lily whispered. 'What happened?'

The dragon twitched its tail, and Lily flinched, as it seemed to be about to destroy several lumps of dustsheeted furniture. But the tail went straight through, as if it wasn't really there. 'Things changed,' it murmured vaguely. 'There was not as much magic in the earth and the air. It made it harder to fly. We were tired...'

'Long sleep,' Henrietta muttered, just loud enough to hear.

The dragon's eyes glittered, and then it laughed, that same rumbling laugh Lily had heard in the night. 'Indeed, little dog.'

'Are you real somewhere, now?' Lily asked. 'It's hard to explain. Is there, I don't know, a cave? Where you're all sleeping?'

The dragon swung his head round to her in surprise, and Lily pressed herself back into the chair instinctively. She suspected that when he was properly real, he would be very much larger – too large to fit in this room, perhaps. But he was big enough now. His eyes were like great, glittering, faceted apples, so close to hers. Lily was sure he was a he, now, she realised.

'We are here.'

'In the carvings?' Lily asked doubtfully, peering round the back of the chair at the fireplace.

The dragon snorted a laugh. 'No. No, I felt you through the stone, that was all. Your strong, delicious magic. You wanted us to be real so very much.'

'Then where?'

'You were almost right. Underneath. The deepest cellars. There are natural hollows and caves all through our territory. Limestone, you see. The house is built on top of a whole lacework of caves. My old self is stretched out by an underground river that comes to the surface further down this valley. Or it did, at least,' he added.

'So much has changed. There seems to be a great deal more of the house than there was.'

'Why have you woken up now? It isn't just because we tried to wake you. I saw you twitching the wings of the dragons on the banisters, and I heard you talking to me. And that was before we tried to bring the carving to life.'

The dragon half-stretched out its wings, so that they scraped the ceiling. Then he tested his claws against the floorboards again. This time, Lily thought there might be the faintest of scratches.

'The magic has come back,' he told her at last. 'I feel strong again.'

'But that doesn't make sense,' Lily told him helplessly. 'No one's doing any magic. It's not allowed. That's why we're here, because we were breaking the law.'

'Think, Lily!' Henrietta growled, leaping on to the arm of the chair. 'No one is doing magic! No spells are using up the magic in the air. That's what he needs to fly, he said so! No one has been doing magic for about twenty years. It's all there, still, sloshing around.' She shivered. 'Who knows what else is going to wake up.'

The dragon nodded. 'It has been happening for a while,' he agreed. 'I have been waking slowly. And then the children came, and there was so much magic, seeping down to us, through the floors, through the stone. Delicious, strong, young magic filling up the Hall again.'

'Magic that no one's allowed to use,' Lily snarled. 'They don't even want to. They think it's evil.'

The dragon blinked slowly. 'Magic is neither good nor evil,' he pointed out, his voice gentle, as though he was teaching a rather stupid child. 'How could it be? It just is. Like wind, or water.'

'Your wings are fading.' Henrietta leaned forward, staring at them closely.

'I am tired again,' the dragon agreed. 'Soon I shall be altogether real, but not yet. Your strong magic is waking me, cousin. These last few days, the blood has quickened in me. It won't be much longer.'

'Then what will you do?' Lily asked, but the dragon was fading faster and faster. If he answered, they could not hear him.

TWELVE

Lily and Henrietta tried again and again to find the dragon over the next few days. But he never returned to the room with the marble overmantel. Lily decided that they must have worn him out, talking to him for so long. She longed to call him back, but she couldn't quite bring herself to summon a three-hundred-year-old legend. It would be presumptuous.

Every so often the dragons around the house fluttered their wings at her, or stretched out their tiny necks to stare at her as she went past. Little serpentine figures seemed to shine out of the carvings, glittering and blinking as she came by. Lily seemed to see more of them whenever she looked. She wasn't sure how. Unless it meant that the other dragons were waking now too.

It wasn't only the carvings. Wherever she went, strange flickering shapes whisked around corners ahead of her. A spiky head even seemed to dart out of the fireplace in the schoolroom once. It eyed the class thoughtfully, stared in fascination at Lily, and wreathed itself around the class as a dragon made of blueish woodsmoke. Everyone coughed, and it reared back in alarm, and then disappeared into the dull glow of the embers.

'They're everywhere,' Lily murmured to Henrietta that night. The pug was hidden under her blankets, half-asleep, and she only grunted in answer.

'They must all be waking up. Don't you see them?' Lily prodded Henrietta's plump side, and she wheezed crossly.

'Of course I do. But they've been haunting this place for centuries, Lily. We're only seeing them now because we know what to look for.'

'You don't think there are more of them?' Lily asked her disappointedly.

'Maybe, maybe not. Tricksy little things. Now be quiet and let me sleep.'

But Lily lay awake. She was sure Henrietta was wrong, there were more dragons now. She could imagine the cavern, deep underneath the house. There had been an old book of engravings of the *Natural*

Beauties of England at Merrythought, an improving volume that had been abandoned in the dusty schoolroom. It had several colour plates of amazing limestone caves, dripping with stalactites. There could have been dragons in those pictures too. The great mounds of glistening rock curled and draped over each other in strangely living shapes.

The dragon upstairs had told them that the caves under Fell Hall were limestone. Sleepily, Lily peopled the caves she remembered from the pictures with huge beasts, their shining bodies still for three hundred years, as they slumbered beside an underground river. That ragged fringe of greenish stalagmites marked the spiked spine of a sleeping dragon. She smiled dreamily to herself. It would be much easier to fight for magic if she knew a flock of friendly dragons.

But they still weren't moving, she realised sadly, as she drifted into a deeper sleep.

The dull routine of Fell Hall was broken the next morning. Lily was half-asleep, and hardly saw what happened. After a night spent dreaming of dragon caverns, waving her arms exactly as Miss Merganser wanted them waved was taking up all her attention. But the girls around her, more awake, and so practised at drill that they didn't have to think, were whispering and scuffling at something down by the lake. Lily blinked, and waited for the next head-turn so that she could peer across to the water.

The Indian club-waving had disintegrated into a knot of unruly boys, staring at the something lying at their feet. Then it resolved itself into a slow procession, carrying a still figure past the girls and on into the house. The figure was Peter. Lily knew it almost as soon as she saw them pick him up.

'A fit,' Mr Fanshawe told Miss Merganser as he came past. 'An outbreak of his magic, clearly. The stupid boy is resisting us.'

Lily swallowed miserably as she watched the boys carry Peter inside. He was greyish pale, and one hand swung limply down from the old rug they'd used as a makeshift stretcher. He wasn't resisting! He didn't have any magic to resist with!

She turned to whisper to Georgie, but her sister wasn't looking at her. She was standing with Sarah, and the two of them were shaking their heads sadly, their lips pursed.

Lily nearly snarled. How could Georgie put on that stupid disapproving face? She *knew* Peter. She knew it wasn't an outbreak of magic. It was the cocoa, or the bluebottle spells, or both.

Peter wasn't at breakfast, but he appeared in lessons,

marched into the schoolroom by Mr Fanshawe, with no more colour in his face than before. He sat slumped before his desk, gazing unseeingly at his hands, which lay slackly on the wood in front of him.

At the end of the class he didn't move, even when the other boys shoved past him. He was like a huge doll, slumping over a little further as his sawdust stuffing sagged.

'Peter!' Lily didn't care any more if the other girls saw her talking to him. 'Peter!' She tried to make him understand, but he wasn't even looking at her. And if he didn't look, he couldn't hear. There was nothing. It was as if he were locked away inside.

'Leave him alone,' Miss Merganser snapped. She did look faintly concerned about the state of Peter, Lily thought. But not nearly as much as she should. He was only an orphan, of course. A foundling. He had no parents who might make a fuss. 'What are you teasing him for? Nasty, unprincipled girl! Get out of my sight!' She hauled Peter up, and he trailed loosely from her hands, only just standing.

Lily fled, but not to the grounds after the others. Instead she raced up the stairs to the room with the overmantel. This time, she wasn't just going to sit and stroke the marble dragon, and hope that he came back. It was too urgent for that. She didn't care how old he was, or how rare, or if she was being rude. She needed him now. She didn't know enough about magic to help Peter, and even if the dragon had been asleep for the last three hundred years, he was a legendary, mythical creature. Dripping with magic. Surely he could tell her what to do.

Henrietta was asleep on the pink velvet chair, and she woke with a start as Lily flung open the door.

'What is it?' she snapped, jumping up. 'Have you done something dreadful?'

'No!' Lily was too worried even to protest. 'It's Peter. I don't know what it is. Too much more of the cocoa, or maybe they tried to make him tell them about Mama. Whatever it was – it's like he's broken. He just isn't there any more. I don't know what to do, and I'm sure they don't either. We need the dragon.'

'What makes you think he'd want to help?' Henrietta sniffed.

Lily shrugged. 'He said it was my magic that helped him wake up. He might be grateful. And if not, perhaps he'll do it on a promise. I'll bind my magic to him, or something like that. A year's service, in exchange for getting us all away from here. He said magic was delicious. He must want more of it.'

Henrietta nodded doubtfully. 'And how are we summoning him?' she enquired, leaping down from the chair to stand in front of the marble dragon.

Lily sighed. 'I haven't worked that part out yet,' she admitted.

'Flattery,' Henrietta suggested. 'It always works on me.'

'What, *O Great Dragon, we beg that you help us*?' Lily wrinkled her nose.

'Exactly. Keep going. And perhaps kneel down, don't you think? And the right voice, Lily. You're begging, remember.'

Lily knelt in front of the carving, holding out her cupped hands. She felt stupid, but she had a feeling Henrietta was right. The dragon had seemed a very formal creature.

'Great Dragon, we beg that you help us. We are in need of your mighty strength, and...' She rolled her eyes at Henrietta for inspiration.

'Awesome claws.'

Lily scowled. 'And your awesome claws.'

'Shining scales.'

'Oh, come on, Henrietta, that's just silly...' Lily turned back to complain, and her voice died away.

'That last bit wasn't me,' Henrietta whispered. The awesome claws were wrapped round her, and the dragon was eyeing her rather hungrily. He was much clearer this time. And bigger. Big and clear enough for Lily to see that his claws were each about Henrietta's own height.

She was sitting in the middle of them, trying not to twitch.

'I do have shining scales,' the dragon told Lily.

'I know,' she whispered. The room was filled with their strange pearly light.

'Why did you call me?'

'I'm sorry…' Lily began.

'Oh, you need not be sorry. Your call seems to help me make the leap back. Most helpful. I am real enough to be hungry now, but I take it you still want the small dog?'

'I do,' Lily agreed hastily. 'Please. We can try to find you something else.'

The dragon nodded thoughtfully. 'Perhaps better to wait a little longer anyway. My insides may not be up to it yet.' He opened his claws, and Henrietta shot out, curling herself into Lily's lap. 'What did you want? I could tell you were in great need. Your invocation was quite heartfelt.' He sounded smug, and Lily realised that Henriettta had been right. Flattery worked.

'One of our friends has been injured, somehow. He doesn't have any magic, but the staff here think that he does, and they're trying to get rid of it. They have spells of their own, awful ones, and they're using them to make us think magic is wrong. I think they went too far with Peter. We don't know how to bring him back.'

The dragon nodded his great head, and his dark eyes glittered. 'Twisting magic inside people's heads is a dangerous business. He isn't the only one. I'll show you.' He turned, more carefully this time, as he was almost solid, and the furniture rocked as he passed it. He had to ease himself carefully through the door, and as he paced down the passageway, Lily was sure she could see the floorboards sagging under his weight. He was awfully close to being real.

What was going to happen, when there was a real dragon in Fell Hall again? Lily wondered for a moment. She had a feeling he wouldn't want to stay cooped up under the house.

The dragon led them across the stairwell to the right-hand passage, the one that Lily had avoided, as it looked more inhabited.

'Someone does live up here then?' she asked, and then yelped, and stuffed her hands across her mouth, as the dragon disappeared through a solid wooden door, like a ghost.

'Follow him!' Henrietta snapped. 'Pick me up, and follow him!'

Several coils of long, shining tail were still vanishing through the door, the one with the elaborate lock that Lily had tried before. Lily watched it, round-eyed. Then she stretched out a hand, and caught one of the dagger-like spikes. Her fingers seemed to sink into it at first, but then it settled, warm and smooth, not at all as she had expected it to be.

Henrietta whined, and Lily shut her eyes as the dragon pulled them after him through the thick door – which melted and gave like butter, dropping them breathless into a dim, heavily furnished room, where an old lady was sitting by a dying fire, and watching them.

Lily swallowed, and bobbed a curtsey. 'Good morning,' she muttered.

The old lady inclined her head politely, as though she couldn't quite help it, but she said nothing.

'She does not believe that you are actually here,' the dragon explained. 'And she cannot see me. She has no magic in her, at all, and I am not yet real enough for her to see me properly.'

'Why doesn't she believe we're here?' Lily whispered back. She felt rude whispering in front of the old lady, but at least she thought they were imaginary.

The old lady shook her head, as though trying to shake away a strange dream, and bent down to put more wood on the fire.

'I have watched what is happening at Fell Hall, since the magic thickened again, and I started to wake up. She has been here a long time, I think. Since before the children came, when I only caught strange glimpses as I dreamed in the caverns below. She thinks that she is mad.'

'She doesn't look mad,' Lily murmured. The old lady was neatly dressed, and wearing a little lace cap. She had clearly been doing embroidery, but had stopped, as her candle had burned down, and the windows were shuttered. The fire was her only light, and the room was too dim to see her stitches, or to read.

'No. But they tell her she is. Always. And now she believes them.'

'Who? Miss Merganser?'

'Yes, and the others before her.' The dragon coiled himself around the old lady's chair, staring up at her sadly. The light from his scales burned brighter, and she smiled suddenly, and picked up her embroidery again.

'She can see your light, then,' Henrietta pointed out. 'Are you sure she can't see you?' she added, peering at the embroidery. Silvery dragons curled and frolicked all over the fabric, delicately constructed from hundreds and hundreds of tiny stitches.

Lily sighed. It was a pity the old lady thought she was imaginary. She could have helped Lily with her needlework. 'She must know about dragons, to sew all these,' she agreed.

The dragon shrugged, and the candelabra in the ceiling swung wildly to and fro. 'She can sense me somehow, I think. But that only makes the poor creature even more certain that she is deranged.' He laid his muzzle on the arm of the old lady's chair, and stared at her fiercely, as though he were willing her to see him. But she only blinked, and carried on sewing.

'This is stupid,' Henrietta snapped, and she jumped on to the old lady's lap, and knocked the basket of embroidery silks on to the floor. Then she looked up at her slyly, as if daring the old lady to call her imaginary.

'You really are a dog,' the old lady murmured, reaching out a thin, papery-skinned hand, as if she would like to stroke Henrietta.

'She won't bite,' Lily promised.

'I might.' But Henrietta wagged her tail as she said it.

'A talking dog…'

Lily had expected the old lady to recoil in horror, but she smiled, and rubbed Henrietta's ears. 'I haven't met anyone like you in a long while. Perhaps you won't like this, but you remind me of a most beautiful and superior cat that I knew long ago.'

Henrietta sniffed disgustedly. 'Some cats are adequate company, I suppose.'

'I really do remember him…' the old lady murmured anxiously.

Lily glanced at the dragon doubtfully. How was she supposed to reassure someone that they weren't mad?

But Henrietta seemed to have taken a fancy to the

old lady, despite her fondness for cats. 'Personally, I don't see why you would want to, but I'm sure you're right. Why are you here?'

'Oh… Because I disagreed with my family. My mind began to fail. I had to be shut away. I forget things, too. I can hardly remember who I am, some days…'

Lily frowned. 'What did you disagree with them about?'

'Magic.' The old lady sighed. 'I rather liked it, you see. I still do,' she added with a touch of defiance.

'And your family sent you away just because of that?' Lily asked indignantly. 'Couldn't you have just been quiet about it? That's what we did, my sister and me. We were caught, but only because we were betrayed. And if you weren't even *doing* any magic…'

'That wasn't good enough,' the old lady sighed. 'I wouldn't renounce it publicly, that was the problem. A symptom of my madness, I think.' But she was frowning now.

'You really don't seem very mad,' Lily told her.

'I've been so confused,' she whispered. 'Strange visions and voices. I have *felt* mad. But these last few weeks, things have been so much clearer. Although,' she dipped her head, shamefaced. 'I do still keep seeing the dragons, so stupid of me. When of course they can't possibly be there.'

'Me,' the dragon murmured. 'She has felt me, when I came to see her. It's clearing her mind.'

Lily was just about to ask him what he meant, when the old lady sat up suddenly straighter, gazing worriedly at Lily. 'You're real, then,' she murmured. 'You are! Dear child, you are in such danger. You should go. Fell Hall does terrible things to children like you. And the poor dog. Please get away from here!'

'What sort of things?' Lily asked, wondering how often Miss Merganser or the others came up to this room, and almost hearing footsteps.

'It hasn't happened for a while. I had wondered if all the strong children had gone – if it had worked, if they had managed to breed the magic out. But not quite yet. It's those dreadful bottled spells. When they fight against strong magic like yours, it has the most terrible effect. They bring the children up here sometimes, afterwards, to the rooms on either side of mine. They need somewhere to keep them, I suppose, though there are other rooms, hidden all round the house, I think. They can't manage to be with the others any more, poor little things. Although they're never here for long. They forget how to be alive, I think. They're so silent – the floorboards never creak. They bring them food, but I never hear them eating, or pouring water. Nothing.'

It sounded horribly like what had happened to Peter,

Lily thought, flinching. That strange blank look on his face. But he didn't have any magic for the spell to fight against, Lily told herself. That couldn't be what they'd done to him. Peter had just had too much of the doctored cocoa. He would come back.

'What did you mean, when you said you were clearing her mind?' she asked, glancing up at the dragon, but then she gasped. He was fading again, the silvery-white light dimming, and they were on the wrong side of a locked door. 'Wait!' she called, but he was already gone, only a few glimmering specks floating in the air to show where he had been.

The old lady's eyes suddenly sharpened anxiously, and she stood up stiffly, her embroidery falling unnoticed to the floor. 'They cannot find you here!' she told Lily. 'You'll have to hide, perhaps you can slip out when the maid brings me food. They mustn't see you!'

For a moment, Lily was infected with the same panic. Her heart raced, and she glanced around the room, searching for a hiding place. Then she laughed. She had used her magic so little at Aunt Clara's house, and here at Fell Hall, she had almost forgotten what she could do. And now she felt so much stronger, as though the dragon had poured life into her magic.

'We'll see you again,' she promised the old lady. 'We'll be very careful, don't worry.' Then she caught

Henrietta up in her arms, and closed her eyes deliciously, loving the warmth of the magic as it crept over her skin on little velvet feet. There were so many things she could do. The grey spells on the house *had* been working on her, she realised, and she hadn't noticed. She'd suddenly remembered that her magic was there after all.

'We could let it take us outside the walls,' Henrietta whispered. 'We'd be free.'

'Not without Georgie,' Lily sighed. 'Or Peter. And I think those walls have other spells in them – I could feel them when Elizabeth was showing us the stone. We couldn't. Not yet, anyway.'

The dormitory, she whispered to the magic inside her, and they saw the old lady's delighted, frightened face as the magic whirled around them, and they disappeared.

THIRTEEN

'Did you hear what he said?' Lily muttered to Henrietta.

Henrietta shook herself, silver shimmering along her smooth black fur. 'Mmm? What? Oh, that was nice, Lily. I've missed magic.'

'I know, we've been stupid, letting Aunt Clara put us off, and then the sneaky spells they've been winding round us here. Henrietta, did you hear the dragon saying he'd been clearing the mind of the old lady upstairs? What do you think he meant?'

Henrietta frowned. 'Let's not talk about it here. I know you girls aren't supposed to be in your dormitory in the daytimes, but there's always someone in and out. And they might be looking for you – weren't you supposed to be in the kitchens all this time?'

Lily nodded, and they hurried to the door, peering round it carefully. 'We'll go out to the gardens, and then try to slip in later. I can say I felt ill.'

'Be careful,' Henrietta murmured. 'I can hide myself quite easily – so many little hidey-holes around this house. But you're a different matter. You mustn't be caught, Lily. Miss Merganser already doesn't like you. You heard what the old lady said. Too many doses of that spell…'

'I know. But I'm sure the dragon could help. He said he was clearing her mind. Perhaps he can bring Peter back? Oh, ssshh, someone's coming.' She darted back behind the door, spying through the crack. 'It's only Georgie. I wonder if she's looking for me?' Lily opened the door, smiling in relief. For once her sister wasn't with Sarah. They would have a chance to tell her what had been happening.

But Georgie was hurrying down the passage, a blank expression on her face. She walked straight past the dormitory door, and didn't seem to see Lily at all.

The words died in Lily's mouth, and she shook. For a moment, she was back at Merrythought, seeing her sister for the first time in weeks – and being ignored. Georgie had been so stuffed full of Mama's magic, and her own fear that she would never be good enough for whatever it was that she was supposed to do. She had forgotten to eat, or wash, let alone pay attention to her little sister.

It wasn't going to happen again.

Lily raced out into the corridor, and seized Georgie's arm, dragging her round.

'Oh! Lily. Where have you been?' She hardly sounded interested, Lily thought furiously. She grabbed Georgie's other hand, and shook her.

'Listen to me!' she snapped.

'Not here,' Henrietta hissed from the doorway, and Lily nodded, pulling Georgie into the linen room, and backing her up against the shelves of greyish blankets, and darned and elderly sheets.

'Lily, we're not allowed in here,' Georgie said crossly. 'We'll get into trouble. And you're already on Miss Merganser's blacklist, Sarah told me.'

'Sarah!' Lily spat crossly. 'Is Sarah your sister now? You haven't spoken to me for days!'

'That isn't true!' But Georgie wouldn't look at her.

'Are you ashamed of me?' Lily demanded.

'Everyone knows you're my sister,' Georgie muttered. 'And you keep doing things...You keep getting into trouble with Miss Merganser.'

'Georgie, why do you care about that?' Lily frowned at her. 'It isn't as if we're staying here! We're getting away, as soon as we possibly can. If it wasn't for the spells embedded in the walls, we would have gone the first night. We have to find Father and get him to destroy the spells inside you. The sooner the better, because I wouldn't put it past those Dysarts to be making trouble for him too.'

Georgie sighed, in a very elder-sisterly way. 'Lily, it's all very well to make plans, but the walls are *there*! We can't get out of this place!' She looked up at Lily. 'And I'm not sure we should be trying to, anyway.'

Lily stared at her. 'What?'

'You want us to find Father so he can get rid of Mama's magic inside me – well, that's what Miss Merganser and everyone here are trying to do, Lily! We need to let them!'

Lily shook her head, slowly. 'You've given in. Henrietta said you would, but I wouldn't believe it. Georgie, they don't want just the bad spells, they'll take everything! And they'll probably turn your mind to custard doing it. Look what they've done to Peter!' She caught her sister's arms, staring into her eyes desperately. 'Georgie, I know your magic frightens you, but you can't let them do this!'

'I have to,' Georgie muttered stubbornly. 'Magic's wrong. You should let them clean yours away too.'

Lily slapped her. She felt ashamed for a second

afterwards, but she was so angry, she couldn't stop herself.

Georgie fell back against a pile of blankets, her hand on her cheek, her eyes watering with the blow.

'I don't want it cleaned! It isn't dirty!' Lily hissed. 'Don't you dare say that! You're a Powers, and magic is part of you. It always will be.' She closed her eyes, feeling the magic in her blood wrapping around her hand. Her fingers stung where she had smacked Georgie – she had probably hurt herself as much as her sister.

Lily lifted her hand again, and Georgie flinched. But this time Lily stroked her sister's cheek, the magic making the scarlet mark across Georgie's pale skin glitter. She could feel the spell on the house resisting her magic, but she wasn't performing any very difficult spells. 'I'm sorry,' she murmured. 'I didn't really mean to do that.' She sank the magic into the mark, and it melted away.

'It's all right,' Georgie said shakily. She put her own hand across Lily's, holding it there. 'I haven't felt any magic for so long. It was lovely.' Her knees seemed to give way, and she sank to the floor, pulling Lily down next to her. 'I'm so stupid,' she murmured. 'It's as if there's a fog all round me, and now the sun's burning it away. I believed them. How could I believe them?'

Lily put her arms around Georgie, holding her

tightly. 'Henrietta reckons it's Mama's spells. You've already been weakened, you see. The cocoa works better on you. It's full of spells, we're sure. Spells to make everyone do as they're told. Henrietta can taste them.'

'Wonderful.' Georgie gave a miserable little laugh. 'I'm useless.'

Lily sighed. 'You aren't. You're just a bit…'

'Broken,' Henrietta put in helpfully, resting her nose on Georgie's knees and staring up at her.

Lily frowned, but Georgie laughed again, a little less bitterly. 'Always so tactful, darling Henrietta.'

'Georgie, we might have found someone who can mend you a little bit,' Lily told her persuasively. 'I don't think he'll be able to get rid of Mama's spells, but he might be able to wash away everything Sarah's been saying.'

'Who?' Georgie stared at her worriedly. 'Lily, what have you been doing?'

Lily patted her cheek again, encouragingly. 'It's all right. We've woken up a dragon, that's all.'

'I'm such a terrible actress,' Georgie whispered, as she sat on Lily's bed, cupping her cocoa in both hands, and taking little pretend sips. 'I almost dropped the mugs, my hands were shaking so much.'

'It's all right. Sarah's so bespelled she wouldn't notice if you'd gone blue in the face, as long as you took both our mugs. Tell me when no one's looking, so I can pour them out of the window.'

'We can't stay here once it gets colder,' Georgie murmured. 'They'll close the windows then.'

'We're not staying anyway,' Lily growled. 'A few more days, that's all. Even if I have to promise him half a treasury.'

'Does he like gold?' Georgie whispered, fascinated.

'Actually, I don't know,' Lily admitted. 'We've only spoken to him a few times. He was quite keen on eating Henrietta, but I'm not really sure what he wants.'

Lily's pillow quivered indignantly.

'I expect she'd be a bit stringy,' Georgie giggled, and Lily glared at her.

'Don't go getting hysterical.'

'I can't help it! A dragon!' Georgie whispered back. 'Honestly, Lily, I go and get myself bespelled for a few days, and you find a dragon. Typical.'

'You'd better go back to your bed, and pretend to be asleep. We have to wait until no one notices us going.' Lily quickly poured both cups of cocoa out of the window.

The other girls were already settling down for the night, but every time Lily thought it was safe to get up, someone else would turn over, or mutter something, and she would have to lie down again, kicking frustratedly at her blankets.

'Lily…' Georgie was sitting up in bed, staring at her. 'Can't we go yet? I'm sure everyone's asleep.'

Lily blinked. The room was quiet, except for the patter of Henrietta's claws, as she trotted up and down, sniffing at each bed. 'She's right. They're all sleeping. Come on!'

Lily slipped out of bed, and followed Henrietta to the door. Georgie's hand slipped into hers, and they made their way to the stairs, hurrying up to the third floor, and the room with the overmantel.

Georgie stroked the carving delicately, smoothing her fingers over the scales. 'Is this what he looks like?' she asked, and Lily nodded. 'Even the colour. I don't know if he was always this sort of silvery blue, or it's just that we used the marble to call him.'

'I am a little larger than that now,' a voice said solemnly, and Georgie squeaked.

Even Lily drew in a sharp breath, and she had seen him before. But now the dragon was enormous, crammed into the room with his spiked spine pressed against the ceiling, and his tail wound in and out of the furniture.

'You may have to start summoning me outside,' the dragon suggested.

Lily nodded. 'Are you real yet?'

'Touch me.'

Lily reached out a hand, and brushed her fingers over his scales. 'You feel real.'

'I thought so too,' he said, sounding pleased. 'All of me is here now. Nothing left down in the cavern. The others are starting to wake too,' he added, twitching his tail and watching it admiringly.

'Others?' Georgie whispered, staring at him. 'There are more of you?'

'Twelve altogether.' He nodded. 'But I don't know if all of them will wake up,' he added, swinging his head from side to side rather unhappily. 'We have been asleep a very long time.'

'Can you appear and disappear still, now you're real?' Lily asked worriedly. She wasn't sure he was ever going to be able to get out of the room, if he couldn't.

'Only in Fell Hall, since I've been here so long. I'm part of the house, so I can disappear through the carvings. If I leave, I shall be solid.' He stretched out his claws. 'But I wouldn't mind that. I've been half a dream for such a very long time.'

Georgie swallowed. 'He'd fit in the theatre, Lily. There's masses of space.'

'The theatre?' The dragon's eyes glittered as he brought his massive head down closer to the girls.

'Where they have plays? There was a troupe of actors at the Hall once.'

'This one has dancing, and songs, mostly,' Lily admitted. 'But recitations sometimes. And very good juggling. Georgie and I were part of an act once.' It seemed a very long time ago. She wondered for a moment if Daniel had found another assistant.

'So if I were to take you away from here, I might be able to stay in this theatre?' the dragon suggested.

Lily nodded slowly. She had been planning to beg him to help them escape. It was rather strange to have him suggest it instead.

He gave a little snort of amusement, and wisps of smoke curled from his huge black nostrils. 'Hmf. A long time since that has happened. Dear little cousin, you do not have to tell me that you need me to help you escape. I can feel you needing it. Your thoughts are buzzing with it.' He lowered his massive head, and stared at Georgie, his saucer-sized eyes gazing into hers.

Georgie stepped towards him, hypnotised by the great, glittering eyes, and Lily swallowed. He had wanted to eat Henrietta. What *did* he eat? Now he seemed so much larger, and so much more solid, it was easier to imagine...

But then Georgie reeled away, her hands flying to her

ears, and staggered across the room to collapse gracefully on a chair.

It's the theatre training, Lily found herself thinking. *She even faints nicely.*

'Better,' the dragon said approvingly. 'Yes, I thought so. Your sister wants to escape too, now those tangled enchantments round her have gone.'

Lily looked hopefully at Georgie, who nodded, making the strangest face, as though she was trying to look down her own nose. 'I think so. I don't feel like I'm under a spell. But then, I didn't before either,' she admitted sadly.

'There's still something else,' the dragon muttered, laying his head along the back of Georgie's chair. 'Something deeper, that I can't quite pull away…'

'Mama's spells,' Lily sighed. She had hoped for a minute that he might have broken those too. But they were too old, and too deep. 'Could you do that to all the children?' she asked him hopefully. 'We'll take you to London. You'd like the theatre, I know you would.'

'It would be busy?' the dragon asked, almost shyly. 'I long for busy, after three hundred years of quiet.'

'Very busy.' Lily laughed, remembering the panic before each night's show.

'Then I will take you there.' The dragon nodded.

'You, and all the others, if they can be persuaded to ride on me.'

'How long is it since you've flown?' Georgie asked him, in a small voice.

The dragon drew up his head proudly – although the gesture was rather spoiled by having to mind the ceiling. 'One does not forget.'

'Oh.' Georgie nodded. 'Good.'

FOURTEEN

'We should go now,' Lily said suddenly. 'Now, before they break any more of us.'

The dragon swung his head to look at her, and the glitter in his dark eyes intensified. He was excited. He wanted to fly, she thought.

'If you want to take the others with you,' Henrietta pointed out, 'we need to get rid of the effects of that cocoa. They're more likely to run screaming from a dragon than want to escape on one, at the moment. Even without those spells, he is still *quite* frightening.'

The dragon yawned, deliberately showing Henrietta the size of his teeth. Lily thought that he probably objected to being only quite frightening.

It was true, though. She could imagine Lottie being

brave enough to climb on to a dragon's back – but the others? Elizabeth and Sarah would run screaming for Miss Merganser. She clenched her fists frustratedly. 'Could you do what you've done for Georgie to all the others? Clear away the spells they've been drugged with?' She frowned. 'It might be harder than it was with Georgie,' she admitted slowly. 'They've all been here longer.'

'I can remove the worst effects,' the dragon agreed. 'There is one room where you all sleep, is there not?'

'All the girls.' Lily nodded. 'The boys are on the other side of the passage.'

The dragon chuckled. 'There is enough of me now. The boys can have the tail end.'

'What will you have to do?' Georgie asked, curiously.

The dragon shrugged a little. 'Nothing. Touch them all perhaps. Be near them. It is very hard to keep someone under a spell with a dragon around. We like magic too much.'

'And it won't hurt you, taking away all those spells?' Lily asked, a little anxiously.

'Hardly.' He gave another dismissive snort, and again, the smoke coiled from his nostrils. Lily, Georgie and Henrietta eyed it, fascinated, but too polite – or too scared – to say anything.

'Oh!' Lily reached out a hand to him. 'The old lady along the passage! We should take her with us too.'

'What?' Georgie asked. 'Lily, have you been all over this house?'

'I was trying to find Peter. And then I heard the dragon whispering to me. I had to explore.'

'While you were drinking your cocoa and doing as you were told,' Henrietta snapped.

'I thought you were trying not to be so mean,' Lily reminded her. 'You'd like her, Georgie. She does the most amazing embroidery. Actually, if we're all going back to the theatre, maybe she can help you and Maria in the wardrobe.'

Georgie brightened at the thought, but then she looked troubled. 'Lily, what are we going to do with all those children? They can't all live at the theatre. And the girls told us that their families would get into trouble if they ran away.'

'But they can't do that for *all* their families, can they?' Lily asked doubtfully.

Georgie shrugged. 'I think the Queen's Men can do anything they like.'

'We can't leave them here,' Lily muttered. 'We just can't.'

'I know.' Georgie shivered. 'I think we're going to find it hard to hide, Lily. The Queen's Men probably know we were at the theatre – Aunt Clara would have told them, surely? Don't worry,' she told the dragon.

'I'm sure you can still hide there.' She smiled. 'They might use you as scenery. Are you good at keeping still?'

'You are being hunted?' he asked curiously.

'We will be, when they find out we've run away from here,' Lily sighed.

The dragon's tail twitched enthusiastically. 'This becomes more and more interesting. We must certainly rescue the old lady, as well. We cannot leave one of her blood here.' He shimmered in the darkness of the room, and melted into a misty outline of a dragon, and then simply a dragon-shaped space, before the light adjusted itself again, and the three of them were alone in the dark.

You will have to come and talk to her, a voice rumbled around Lily's ears. *She is still not quite sure about me.* Lily shook herself.

'What did he mean, one of her blood?' Henrietta growled, as they hurried along the passage.

'I haven't any idea,' Lily admitted. It had sounded sinister, someone with such large teeth discussing blood.

The door to the old lady's room was open, and she was standing in the middle of it, looking rather shaken, and dressed only in a delicate, lace-edged nightgown, and a cap. There was no doubt that she could see the dragon now. But she wasn't screaming. She was quite calm, though very pale. Lily was sure her eyes were brighter, in the shining light of the dragon.

It was as though a film of sleep had been lifted from them.

'She is far too special to be left behind,' the dragon told Lily, his voice deep and caressing.

Lily frowned at him. 'Why? What did you mean about her blood?'

The dragon blinked at her, the lids closing slowly over his great eyes. 'Dragons have always had an affinity for royal blood,' he explained, as though to a simpleton. 'Her presence has helped to waken me too, I am sure.'

'Royal blood?' Georgie stared at the old lady, and Henrietta went to sniff her ankles suspiciously.

'Fifty years gone, since I met any princesses,' she muttered, still sniffing. 'One of the present queen's sisters, perhaps.'

'Her younger sister.' The old lady inclined her head politely. 'Princess Jane. Tell me. The dragon.' She didn't look at him, merely waved a hand behind her at his silvery bulk, and swallowed. 'He is here? I'm not hallucinating?'

'No, indeed, Your Highness.' Georgie curtseyed, and glared at Lily until she did the same.

Lily bobbed her knees ungracefully, staring all the while. 'But if you're a princess, what are you doing here? Oh! That's why it mattered that you wouldn't say publicly that you renounced all magic. You mean your own sister shut you up in here? Queen Sophia?'

'It was my mother more, I think, Queen Adelaide, the Dowager Queen,' Princess Jane explained. She seemed to have relaxed, strangely, now she knew there really *was* a dragon in her bedroom. 'She was so angry, after poor Papa was murdered by that magician. One could understand why. But I never saw why one madman meant we had to destroy all magic. It was so beautiful. I knew several magicians. I had a magician girl as my maid for a while, to protect me from another plot. She was a Fell too, it turned out in the end.'

'What happened to her, after the Decree?' Lily whispered.

'Rose? She went to the Americas. Many of our magicians did. Magic isn't outlawed there. She wrote to me for a while – perhaps she still does.' The old princess sighed.

'We saw your sister, in London,' Lily told her, and the old lady's face brightened. She caught Lily's hand, and pulled her to the little sofa. The dragon curled himself around them, listening avidly. He went all round the sofa easily now, with his tail coiling round all over again.

'Tell me, is she well?'

Lily frowned, and glanced at Georgie. 'She didn't look very happy,' she admitted. 'We only saw her from a distance, in a carriage. But she looked – burdened.'

Princess Jane nodded. 'Poor Sophia,' she murmured. 'She has such a strong sense of duty. And she is so much under Mama's control.'

'I think your mama is madder than you are,' Henrietta jinked her way between the dragon's claws, and jumped up beside the old princess.

Princess Jane grimaced. 'Well. Let us say that she is very determined.' It sounded as though she were agreeing.

'Does your sister know where you are?' Lily asked hesitantly.

'I think not.' The princess sighed. 'She is very tender-hearted. Mama would not have told her that I was shut away somewhere like this.'

'So it's really your mother who hates magic so much?'

'She never liked it,' Princess Jane admitted. 'After Papa was killed, she was distraught. Maddened, even, as you say. Sophia could never have stood up to her, and she was grieving too. By then Lucasta and Charlotte, my other sisters, were both married, and living abroad. It was only Sophia and Mama and me at the palace – and Mama's legions of advisers, every one of them encouraging her to believe that all magic was evil.'

'Why didn't you just go along with them?' Georgie

asked. She was envious of the princess's strength of mind, Lily realised sadly. 'Wouldn't it have been easier? You could have gone and lived somewhere away from the palace, and not had to be part of it.'

Princess Jane shook her head. 'Rose saved my life. How could I let them say she was a criminal? Rose, and Bella, and Frederick, and Bella's father. They were people. Not some dreadful stain on our country's history. You must never let them call you that.' She sounded stern, and royal, for the first time.

'We won't,' Georgie murmured, but she sounded rather ashamed.

'Would you help us?' Lily asked slowly. She had never thought of trying to change the way her world worked – magic had been forbidden since before she'd been born. She could hardly imagine a world where it was free again. It made her feel dizzy to think of it.

'We could fight them.' She paused. 'But we have to find our father first. We need him, you see, to help Georgie.'

Georgie was shaking her head frantically, and Lily realised that it probably wasn't tactful to tell the princess that Georgie was full of wrong magic, set to destroy Queen Sophia in the very same way that her father had been assassinated.

She compromised on half the truth. 'Our mama

twisted Georgie's magic. She's under a sort of spell, now.'
Lily smiled sadly at the princess. 'Your mama reminded
me of ours, when I saw her. Ours is very – determined,
too. She hates the way things are now. She's been
fighting against the Queen's Men all along,' Lily
admitted, watching the princess anxiously.

But Princess Jane only smiled. 'It would be foolish to
think that there wasn't a resistance. It's why they have
been so harsh, all this time. But the children – that was
a step too far, taking the children.'

I'm ending up on the same side as Mama, Lily realised
suddenly. Except she wanted to talk to the queen, not
murder her. But after what they had seen at Fell Hall,
she and Georgie couldn't simply go back to hiding, and
letting the Queen's Men break the magic out of children.
They had to bring magic back.

'Once we've found our father – and we think we
know where he is – and he's helped us restore Georgie's
magic…' She paused. 'We could protest…' she said
eventually. 'It's what Father was trying to do, before he
was arrested. He got put in prison for it. For refusing to
deny his magic.'

Princess Jane smiled. 'Much like me.'

'If you were with us too… Do you think we could
ever bring it back?' Lily whispered, the magic suddenly
rushing and thumping in her veins.

The princess patted her cheek with papery old fingers, and sighed. 'We could try. I haven't seen the world for forty years, but even before I was shut up here, it was as though the colour was all seeping away, without the magic. We could try...' She smiled wistfully, and then her eyes sharpened again. 'Is your father in Archgate?'

Lily simply stared at Princess Jane, her mouth dropping open a little.

'Archgate?' Georgie whispered, her eyes widening in hope.

'Oh...' The princess shook her head. 'It's so long since I've talked about these things. I'd forgotten that you wouldn't know.' She sighed. 'It's one of the deep secrets. Known only to the family, and a few of our closest counsellors. Or so it was, anyway.'

'Is that the name of the magicians' prison? Archgate?' Lily laid her hand on the princess's arm, beseechingly. 'That's what we came here to find! The prison. That and to rescue our friend,' she added sadly, thinking of Peter's blank eyes.

'Do you know where it is?' Henrietta scratched at the princess's nightgown imperiously.

'Of course. Where it says.' The princess smiled. 'Archgate. The gate in the arch. You get to it from the huge white marble arch at the front of the palace.'

Lily shook her head slowly. 'We've not been there. But that sounds rather obvious. Are you sure?'

'It's a secret gate. Magically sealed,' the princess explained. 'You can only get in – only even see the door – if you have royal blood, or a warrant from the queen.'

'Oh.' Lily nodded. That sounded more believable. More like something to fight against. 'So – *you* could open the door?'

'Well, yes. I suppose so. I've never actually tried,' the princess agreed thoughtfully. 'But I still have royal blood, even if I am a prisoner.'

'And you'd do that?' Georgie slipped off the sofa, catching the princess's hands in her own, and kneeling before her. 'You'd do it? You'd help us free him? Free me from Mama's spells?'

Princess Jane nodded slowly. 'Everything's so much clearer now.' She ran a gentle hand over one of the fearsome-looking spikes that lined the dragon's spine. 'It's you, isn't it, taking away the spells I've been under? Why should I stay shut up here? I should have fought!' She shook herself. 'I wonder how long those spells have been wrapped around my mind? I should have fought long before. My mother and her counsellors have been using stale, dark magic to suppress us all…'

'And now the real magic is rising again,' Lily whispered. 'It's coming back. It must be – you prove it, don't you?' she asked the dragon.

The dragon flexed his long claws thoughtfully. 'I imagine so. I could not have woken without strong magic flowing through the land.'

'Why did you fall asleep under Fell Hall in the first place?' Lily frowned. 'No one even believes that dragons really existed now!'

The silvery-blue wings shuddered in a dragon-shrug. 'We were old. Tired. We had been awake long enough, and there was no Fell child to fly with. The bloodline was dying out.' He nuzzled thoughtfully at Lily, his huge scales surprisingly soft. 'I still think there's Fell blood in you, child. And your sister. One of the traveller Fells must have come back from the Indies, perhaps, and brought fresh blood into the line, after we'd hidden ourselves away. It's taken a great surge of magic to wake us again. All these young magicians, their power coursing through the stones of Fell Hall, unused.' He chuckled. 'What did they expect? We'll fly with you now, dear ones.'

Lily rested her cheek against the warm scales. They were going to fly. Magic suddenly seemed so much more possible. Irresistible, even. Georgie was leaning against her, stroking the dragon's neck. He was making a strange purring sound, a soft, deep roar that made Lily's teeth buzz.

'We should go back to the dormitory,' Georgie said reluctantly at last, pulling her hand away. 'If someone wakes, and we're not there…'

Lily nodded.

'I shall stay here a while.' The dragon coiled tighter around the princess's little sofa, like a guard dog, and she reached out a cautious hand to stroke his enormous muzzle. He half-closed his eyes with pleasure, and he was more like a dog than ever.

A change from palace lapdogs, Lily thought, almost laughing. But then she remembered that the princess hadn't had even a dog to keep her company up here, and the laugh died. Perhaps the dragon had been all that kept her sane, even if she thought he was a hallucination.

'I will come down to your sleeping rooms soon,' the dragon promised. 'And tomorrow…' He fluttered his wings, the soft blue-white membrane glistening in the darkness.

Lily swallowed. She found herself looking at him in terms of handholds, and there weren't very many.

'Soon.' She nodded, and they crept away down the passage, making for the stairs.

The house was silent, but she knew that the staff patrolled the passages at night. They had stuffed their pinafores and a couple of old blankets into their beds, to make them look occupied from the doorway.

Hopefully it would be enough.

The passages were empty and silent, and they had almost reached the dormitory – perhaps that was why they had dropped their guard.

'Someone's coming!' Henrietta suddenly hissed, and Lily and Georgie stopped short. There was nowhere to hide – no doors, and they could hear the footsteps now. Tapping and pattering, little sharp heels. Miss Merganser.

'Not now!' Lily whispered in a panic. 'She can't! If she spells us now… We have to leave tomorrow. Even the dragon wouldn't be able to undo one of those really strong spells before the morning.' She turned frantically this way and that, but there was nowhere to hide, and down here the spells were still hindering her magic. She couldn't transport them away.

'Call him!' Georgie whispered. 'Perhaps he can hide us – he said he could use the carvings.'

'Not for us…' Lily moaned. But she tried anyway. *Help! She's going to catch us!*

There was a glowing light approaching – a lantern, carried by someone just around the corner.

A little carved figure in the panelling seemed to squirm, just a strange little movement in the half-light of the corridor. But it meant he was there.

Hide us! Please! Lily begged.

I cannot. But I can do other things. Watch. The dragon's rumbling laugh surrounded them for a second, and then the wood shook again. But this time it wasn't the carvings twitching.

A hole had opened at the base of the panelling, and Lily shrank back against the window on the other side of the passage, pulling Georgie with her. Henrietta pressed against their feet, her lips drawn over her teeth, and her tail vibrating with disgust.

A stream of rats was pattering out of the hole, their whiskers twitching from side to side, little dark eyes glinting in the approaching light. One of them stared round at the girls and Henrietta, who breathed the merest breath of a growl, before they scritched away around the corner of the passage.

There was a sharp, horrified scream, and the lantern smashed to the floor, the light dying instantly. The girls shot for the dormitory door, lit by a silvery-white glow from the panelling.

The dragon was stretched out between the beds waiting for them, an amused look in his glittering eyes.

'A sufficient diversion?' he murmured. 'You had better get into bed. I doubt if she will stir from her room before morning, but still.'

His pearly light was filling the room now, casting a delicate gleam on the girls' faces as they slept.

Little Lottie turned over, sighing and smiling in her sleep, and reaching out one hand, as though to stroke something.

The dragon purred with laughter, and nudged his massive head up against her fingers. 'Not that this one needs much help,' he murmured. 'Her power is still sleeping, but she'll be strong, when she's older. Delicious magic.'

'What about the boys?' Lily whispered, thinking of Peter.

'Ah well.' The dragon smiled, and looked around, and Lily gasped.

There were more of them. Still only half there, thin and dreamlike in the darkness. Long, coiling shapes, in every shade. A curious midnight-blue face appeared over the end of Lily's bed, and Henrietta glared at it.

'They will see to the boys,' the dragon explained. 'They are not quite awake yet, but they are strong enough to lift a simple spell. So go to sleep, dear little cousin. When you wake tomorrow, we shall fly for London.'

FIFTEEN

Lily woke slowly to a muttering all around her. She was tired after being up so much of the night, and she had dreamed strange dragon dreams, so it took a moment to remember what had really happened. A moment longer to realise what must be happening now.

She sat up, staring around the dormitory, and Georgie climbed sleepily on to her bed, sitting at the end of it with her nightgown tucked around her feet.

The rest of the girls were gathered into anxious little knots, heads together, whispering. The dragons had gone, but Lily could feel that they were close by and waiting.

Elizabeth and her friends were gathered in the middle of the dormitory, but they turned to look at Lily and Georgie as they saw that Lily was awake. Lottie had bounced out of bed, and now she was leaning on the end of Lily's bed too.

'What's wrong, Lizzie?' she asked her sister.

Elizabeth shook her head. Lily had never seen her look quite so unsure of herself. 'Everything feels – odd,' she murmured. 'Lily, what have you done?'

'Why does everyone always blame me?' Lily muttered.

'Well, you did tell us you'd done spells before,' Lottie pointed out chirpily. 'None of *us* ever have. Though I'd ever so much like to, and I don't care what you say, Lizzie.'

'I have too,' Elizabeth whispered. 'By accident. But I liked it.' She looked round at the others defiantly, as though she expected them to shrink away from her in horror.

'Can it really be all that bad?' Mary asked hesitantly.

'It's worked,' Henrietta told Lily, wriggling out from under her blankets, and eyeing the girls thoughtfully.

'Oh, Lily, you've got a dog,' Lottie squeaked delightedly. She hadn't heard Henrietta talking.

Henrietta pranced down the bed, and allowed Lottie to make a fuss of her, and gradually Elizabeth and the rest of her little gang came closer and stroked her too. Henrietta looked up at Lily, and Lily knew what she was asking. She nodded.

'A little lower, if you please, there's an itchy spot, just there…'

The girls stared at her, and Henrietta looked up at Mary. 'Yes, you were almost there. Just a little lower. Please.'

Silently, Mary did as she was told, and Henrietta panted happily, showing off her long pinkish-purple tongue. 'Perfect,' she told Mary, licking her gratefully. Then she looked round at the others sideways. 'I'm an abomination, according to Mr Fanshawe,' she said chattily. 'Miss Merganser would have me drowned.'

The rest of the dormitory was gathering closer now, staring wide-eyed at the talking dog.

'They'd probably drown *us*, if they knew what we'd been doing,' Lily said quietly.

'What have you been doing?' Sarah asked her. She looked dazed. She had been so strongly under the control of the spells that she even seemed to have trouble walking straight.

'Do you know the history of Fell Hall?'

Most of the girls shook their heads, but Sarah blinked. 'My mother told me once that the Fells were one of the great magical families. She even said…' Sarah tailed off, as though she didn't want to be laughed at for repeating it.

'About the dragons?' Lily suggested.

'I dreamed about a dragon last night!' Lottie bounced

up and down on Lily's bed. 'A huge enormous dragon, and I stroked him!'

'I thought you were more than half awake, little one,' an amused voice said behind them, and the girls turned round slowly, clutching at each other's hands.

'That's what we've been doing,' Henrietta said proudly. 'Lily woke him up.'

The dragon seemed to have shrunk himself a little. He wasn't filling the dormitory the way he had the night before. But he was still large.

The little crowd of girls backed themselves up against the wall, staring, and the dragon stared back. He kept his jaws closed, which Lily thought was tactful.

'He took away the spells you were under,' Lily explained. 'I think he ate them, actually. They were in the cocoa. Miss Merganser and the others were feeding them to you every night.'

'But they aren't allowed,' Sarah murmured, still staring at the dragon. '*We* aren't allowed…'

'I think they bend the rules.' Lily shrugged. 'How else could they control magicians, if not by magic? You knew about the blue bottles, anyway.'

The girls blinked, and Sarah nodded. 'I suppose we did…'

'That isn't fair,' Elizabeth's dark-haired friend muttered.

'The dragons woke up because there's so much unused magic around now,' Lily explained.

'There is.' Lottie nodded. 'I can feel it. And taste it!' She put out her little pink pointed tongue, as though she was licking the air.

'Lottie!' Elizabeth scolded. 'That's rude!'

Lottie grinned at her sister wickedly. 'Watch, Elizabeth…' She closed her eyes, and clenched her fists, her nose wrinkling as she concentrated.

The dragon stretched his neck towards her, purring again. 'Almost, little one! Concentrate…'

'There!' Lottie flicked her fingers, and squeaked in triumph, as a flight of tiny rose-pink birds suddenly fluttered out of nowhere, and went cheeping all around the room. Lottie laughed delightedly, and the other girls stared. Some of them might never have seen real magic, Lily realised, only the cruel binding spells the school used. This was something entirely different, a spell done out of the pure joy of magic.

'Very well done, child.' The dragon nodded approvingly. There were tiny pink feathers around his jaws, Lily noticed. She hadn't counted the birds…

He caught her staring, and ducked his head a little, with an apologetic, sideways glance. When he looked up again the feathers had all gone.

'I wonder if I could do that too…' Elizabeth

murmured, gazing at her little sister, an almost jealous look in her eyes.

'You did magic before,' Lily reminded her. 'That's why you were sent here. But Lottie never drank the cocoa – and she gave you hers. It might take a little longer for all the suppression spells to wear off, that's all.'

'You're going to be awfully hard to hide,' Lottie said to the dragon suddenly. She was still fluttering her fingers, staring at them lovingly. 'No one will be able to say magic doesn't happen any more, when they see a dragon.'

'Where is he going to go?' Elizabeth whispered.

'London.' Lily smiled at him. 'And he'll take us with him, if we want to go.'

'You mean, escape?' Sarah asked, her eyes widening. 'Run away from Fell Hall?'

Lily nodded. 'I know it's difficult. With your families…'

Mary sniffed. 'I don't have a family. I'll go.'

'I don't think ours would take us back anyway,' Elizabeth said miserably, stroking Lottie's arm. 'They haven't written. And they were so ashamed, when we were taken.'

'I think – I hope – we have somewhere to go in London,' Lily explained. 'A theatre. Anyone who can't go back home could stay with us there. We might not be able to stay long,' she added, with a tiny sigh. 'People were chasing us. But you'll be safe.'

'Others are stirring, elsewhere in the house,' the dragon said, flattening his muzzle against the floorboards, and turning a huge dark eye up to Lily. 'If we're going, we must go.'

'Oh! The boys!' Lily jumped off the bed, and hurried to the door, to find it opening as she came closer. She hung back, suddenly sure that Miss Merganser had discovered them. The magic rushed into her fingers, struggling against the damping spell that still lingered in the stones of the walls.

But a boy's face peered round the door, his eyes bulging as he took in the dragon, his wings half open as he prepared to leap after Lily.

'I dreamed about him,' he muttered, and he flung the door open so that the rest of the boys could follow him – even Peter, hauled along by two of the others.

'He was flying us out of here, in my dream,' the boy added doubtfully to Lily.

'Now, if you like,' the dragon agreed. 'Lily, go and fetch the princess from upstairs. I have left her door open for you. We will meet you in the long gallery, round two corners from here. You know it? I can break out of that arched window at the end.'

Lily nodded, and pushed her way through the boys clustered in the doorway, Henrietta racing after her, and snapping at their heels. 'Move! Idiots! Can't you see we have a mission?'

After a dragon, and a princess, the boys hardly seemed to blink at a talking dog, but they flattened themselves against the wall obediently.

As she hurried down the passage, Lily could see the dragon emerging from the dormitory after her, already with children climbing up his back, searching anxiously for handholds. She raced away, dashing for the stairs. It was still only early, but Miss Merganser and Miss Ann would be coming to wake them all soon.

The princess was standing at the top of the stairs, peering worriedly down, and clutching a basket that Lily guessed contained her embroidery.

'You came – he said you would. Is it now?'

Lily nodded breathlessly. 'We have to hurry.'

'What are you doing? Lily Powers! I might have known!'

Lily whirled round, the colour draining from her cheeks. Not now! Not when they were almost away!

'Run!' Princess Jane ran down the stairs faster than any old lady should have been able to, and seized Lily's hand as Miss Merganser strode along the passageway in her sharp-heeled boots. Their tapping seemed to mesmerise Lily. She was fixed to the spot, her hand resting on the carved banister rail, watching the warden approach. The sweetly pretty face was white with anger, the pink lips set into a cruel line.

Something bit her, and Lily jumped, tearing her eyes from Miss Merganser at last, and staring down at the banister.

A tiny wooden dragon glared back and hissed, its wings flapping as though it meant to pull itself out of the carving, and fly away too.

Lily gasped. 'We have to fly!' She turned, hand in hand with the princess, and they stumbled down the next flight of stairs. Lily could hear Miss Merganser tapping down behind them. Closer and closer. She didn't dare look round, just pulled the old princess down the passageways, hoping that she knew the room the dragon had meant. She almost laughed with relief as she turned the final corner – his shining tail was trailing out into the passage. She ran her fingers along it lovingly as they raced into the room.

'She's here!' Georgie cried. 'Lily, climb on!'

'We're being chased!' Lily screamed. 'Miss Merganser! Go now!' She flung herself forward, hauling the princess after her.

The dragon's shining whiteness was hidden now by children, clutching odd garments, and here and there a treasured toy that had survived Fell Hall. He was huge again, stretching the full length of the gallery, large enough for forty children to find handholds along the ragged spikes of his spine. She counted them as she pelted past – all the girls, Lottie with Elizabeth's arms wrapped around her. Twenty boys, was that right? Peter was up near the dragon's front legs, blinking in bewilderment. He was still half-trapped in the spells, Lily realised anxiously. But perhaps the journey on the dragon's back would wash the last of them away.

'Here, Lily,' the dragon called. 'Bring the princess, and sit here, up by my neck.' He shot out one enormous clawed foot, pushing them up on to his back. They had hardly settled themselves in the hollows between the spikes before he hunched his wings for the jump.

Lily could feel his muscles bunching under her. She wrapped her arms tightly around his massive neck. Now that the dragon was larger, the huge plates of his scales were so ridged that she could grip on to them with her bare toes.

'Go,' she panted. 'Hurry!'

One of the littler girls screamed as Miss Merganser appeared in the doorway, her eyes angry blue pits as she took in the dragon, and his load.

'Now,' the dragon muttered, and he swung his

enormous head at the oriel window, smashing the thin stone traceries that held the glass in place, and growling with satisfaction as he caught the scent of the outer air.

He roared as he plunged out of the gaping hole he'd left, drawing his wings tightly in to his sides, and then shooting them out with a desperate lunge as he hurled himself into the air.

They seemed to hang there for a moment, fighting the thinness of the air, and Lily closed her eyes, convinced that they were about to fall.

And then the wings stretched out fully with a sharp, satisfied snap, and they beat, once and then again. There was a rush of air past Lily's ears, and she dared to open her eyes.

There was a great pearly expanse of wing on either side of her, shining in the early morning sun, like the insides of the shells she'd picked up so long ago on the shingle at Merrythought. They had to be as wide as he was long, she realised, blinking. She had never seen them stretched out.

They were spiralling, up around Fell Hall, gaining height, and below them she could see little figures spilling out on to the grass, staring up.

'They'll try to throw spells at us,' she screamed at the dragon, the wind whipping her words away. 'They know we're escaping!'

'Higher soon,' he gasped back, beating his wings ever harder. 'Won't catch us.'

They spiralled higher, and then shot forward, lifted on an air current, like some huge bird of prey.

Behind her there came a sudden, surprised noise, not quite a sigh, and Lily glanced round.

'Peter!' she screamed, and she saw Georgie stretching out desperately, her fingertips scrambling at the old jacket he'd flung on over his nightgown. But she couldn't reach him, and he was tumbling through the air beneath them, his hands convulsing as if he was trying to find some way to hold on to nothing.

'He fell!' she screamed to the dragon. 'He fell, can't you catch him?'

The dragon was peering round, stalling in the air, and falling in sickening jerks.

'Him or us,' he muttered, beating up again. 'I cannot. I would never get airborne again. And they are throwing spells at us, look. If I go lower, they will bring us down.'

Peter was smaller and smaller now, falling horribly fast towards the velvet grass.

Lily leaned forward against the dragon's neck, tears burning her eyes. It seemed so unfair, when she had found Peter again, after so long. How could she lose him now, so carelessly?

'Lily, look!' Georgie screamed, and Lily pulled her

head up, her hair tangling across her eyes with wind and tears, and gasped.

Fell Hall was shaking.

The walls shuddered, and the tiny figures on the terrace seemed to mill around like ants pouring out of a nest.

Exploding out of the dust of the collapsing house came another dragon, red-gold, and another and another.

A dark blue-black creature twirled in a delighted somersault, and shot underneath the falling boy. Lily caught her breath – did the black dragon even understand what was happening? Had it seen Peter, or was it just glorying in the feel of the air on its wings?

With another lazy twist, the dragon darted up towards the boy, catching him like a cat patting at a mouse, and then bounding further up into the sky after them.

'The others!' Lily shrieked to the dragon. 'They're awake! They're here! And one of them caught Peter.'

The dragon glanced back, and nodded. 'Good.' His wings beat more strongly again. 'Very good. London, then, little cousin?'

And Lily nodded, smiling as the wind from his wings streamed her hair behind her. They had done it. They'd rescued Peter, and they had the secret they'd been searching for. And they were flying! The Derbyshire hills rolled beneath them as they sped onwards, and it was too exciting, too wonderful to worry about breaking into a magicians' prison, guarded by who-knew-what. She rubbed one massive scale on the dragon's neck, and nodded again.

'London.'

Read on for an exciting extract
of the first ROSE book . . .

Rose peered out of the corner of the window at the street below, watching interestedly as two little girls walked past with their nursemaid. They were beautifully dressed in matching pale pink coats, and she found them fascinating. How could anyone keep a pink coat clean? She supposed they just weren't allowed to see dirt, ever. The little girls strolled sedately down the street, and Rose stretched up on tiptoe to get one last look as they turned the corner. The bucket she was standing on rocked and clattered alarmingly, and she jumped down in a hurry, hoping no one had heard. The tiny, leaded windows at St Bridget's Home for Abandoned Girls were all very high up, so that the girls were not tempted to look out of them. If any of the matrons realised that Rose had discovered a way to see out, they would do their utmost to stop her, in case her virtue was put at risk by the view of the street. Perhaps they would even outlaw buckets, just in case.

Rose straightened her brown cotton pinafore, and trotted briskly along the deserted passageway to the storeroom to return the bucket. She stowed it carefully on one of the racks of wooden shelves, which was covered in more buckets, brushes and cloths. If anyone saw her, she was planning to say that she had been polishing it.

'Pssst! Rose!' A whisper caught her as she headed for the storeroom door, and Rose shot round, her back against the wall, still nervous.

A small greyish hand beckoned to her from under the bottom shelf, behind a large tin bath. 'Come and see!'

Rose took a deep breath, her heartbeat slowing again. No one had seen her unauthorised use of the bucket. It was only Maisie. 'What are you *doing* under there?' she asked, casting a worried look at the door. 'You'll get in trouble. Come on out.'

'Look,' the whispery voice pleaded, and the greyish fingers dangled something tempting out from under the shelf.

'Oh, Maisie.' Rose sighed. 'I've seen it before, you

know. You showed it to me last week.' But she still crouched down, and wriggled herself under the shelf with her friend.

It was Sunday afternoon. At St Bridget's that meant many of the girls had been in Miss Lockwood's parlour, viewing the Relics. Rose didn't have any Relics, which was why it was a good time for borrowing buckets. Even if anyone saw her, they would probably be too full of silly dreams to care.

'Do you think it's meant to hold a lock of hair?' Maisie asked wistfully. 'Or perhaps a likeness?'

Rose stared thoughtfully at the battered tin locket. It looked as though it had been trodden on, and possibly buried in something nasty, but it was Maisie's most treasured possession – her only possession, for even her clothes were only lent.

'Oh, a likeness, I'm sure,' she told Maisie firmly, wrapping an arm round her friend's bony shoulder. Really she had no idea, but she knew Maisie dreamed about that locket all week, and the hour on Sunday when she got to hold it was her most special time, and Rose couldn't spoil it for her.

'Maybe of my mother. Or perhaps it was hers, and she had my father's picture in it. Yes, that would have been it. I bet he was handsome,' Maisie said dreamily.

'Mmmm,' Rose murmured diplomatically. Maisie

wasn't ugly, exactly, but she was very skinny, and no one looked beautiful with their hair cropped short in case of lice. It was hard to imagine either of her parents as handsome.

All Rose's friends spent Sundays in a dream world, where they were the long-lost daughters of dukes who would one day sweep them away in a coach-and-four to reclaim their rightful inheritance.

Strangely though, unlike all the other girls, Rose did not dream. She had no Relic to hang her dreams on, but that wasn't the main reason. Quite a few of the others didn't either, and it didn't hold them back at all. Rose just wanted to get out of St Bridget's as soon as she possibly could. It wasn't that it was a bad place – the schoolmistress read them lots of improving books about children who weren't lucky enough to have a Home. They lived on the streets, and always went from Bad to Worse in ways that were never very clearly explained. Girls at St Bridget's were fed, even though there was never enough food to actually feel full, only just enough to keep them going. They had clothes, even a set of Sunday best for church, and the yearly photograph. The important thing was, they were trained for domestic service, so that when they were old enough they could earn their own living. If Rose dreamed at all, that was what she dreamed of. She didn't want to be a lady in a big house. She'd settle for being allowed to clean one, and be paid for it. And perhaps have an afternoon off, once a month, although she had no idea what she would do.

Occasionally, girls who'd left St Bridget's came back to show themselves off. They told giggly tales of being admired by the second footman, and they had smart outfits that hadn't been worn by six other girls before them, like Rose's black Sunday dress and coat. She knew because the other girls' names had been sewn in at the top. Two of them even had surnames, which was very grand. Rose was only Rose, and that was because the yellow rose in Miss Lockwood's tiny garden had started to flower on the day she'd been brought to St Bridget's by the vicar. He'd found her in the churchyard, sitting on the war memorial in a fishbasket, and howling. If Rose had been given to dreaming like the others, she might have thought that it meant her father had been a brave soldier, killed in a heroic charge, and that her dying mother couldn't look after her and had left her on the war memorial, hoping that someone would care for a poor soldier's child. As it was, she'd decided her family probably had something to do with fish.

Rose hated fish. Although of course in an orphanage, you ate what there was, and anyone else's if you got half a chance. She knew no grand lady was going to sweep into the orphanage and claim her as a long-lost daughter. It must have been a bad year for fish, that was all. It didn't bother her, and just made her all the more determined to make a life for herself outside.

'What do you think they were like?' Maisie asked pleadingly. Rose was good at storytelling. Somehow her stories lit up the dark corners of the orphanage where they hid to tell them.

Rose sighed. She was tired, but Maisie looked so hopeful. She settled herself as comfortably as she could under the shelf, tucking her dress under her feet to keep warm. The storeroom was damp and chilly, and smelled of wet cleaning cloths. She stared dreamily at the side of the tin bath, glistening in the shadows. 'You were two, weren't you, when you came to St Bridget's?' she murmured. 'So you were old enough to be running about everywhere… Yes. It was a Sunday, and your parents had taken you to the park to sail your boat in the fountain.'

'A boat!' Maisie agreed blissfully.

'Yes, with white sails, and ropes so you could make the sails work, just like real ones.' Rose was remembering the illustrations from *Morally Instructive Tales for the Nursery*, which was one of the books in the schoolroom. The two little boys who owned the boat in the original story fought about who got to sail it first, which obviously meant that one of them drowned in the fountain. Most of the books in the schoolroom had endings like that. Rose quite enjoyed working out the exact point when the characters were beyond hope. It was usually when they'd lied to get more jam.

'You were wearing your best pink coat, but your mother didn't mind if you got it wet.' Rose's voice became rather doubtful here. She hadn't been able to resist putting in the pink coat but really, it was too silly…

Suddenly she realised that Maisie was gazing longingly at the side of the tin bath. 'Yes, look, it's got flower-shaped buttons! Are they roses, Rose?'

Rose gulped. 'I'm not sure,' she murmured, staring wide-eyed at the picture flickering on the metal. 'Daisies, I think…' Had she done that? She knew her stories were good – she was always being bothered for them, so they must be – but none of them had ever come with pictures. Pictures that *moved*. A tiny, plump, pretty Maisie was jumping and clapping as a nattily dressed gentleman blew her boat across a sparkling fountain. *White trousers!* Rose's matter-of-fact side thought disgustedly. *Has this family no sense?*

'Oh, the picture's fading! No, no, bring it back, Rose! I want to see my mother!' Maisie wailed.

'Ssssh! We aren't meant to be here, Maisie, we'll be caught.'

Maisie wasn't listening. 'Oh, Rose, it was so pretty! *I* was so pretty! I want to see it again—'

'Girls!' A sharp voice cut her off. 'What are you doing in here? Come out at once!'

Rose jumped and hit her head on the shelf. The picture promptly disappeared altogether, and Maisie burst into tears.

'Come out of there! Who is that? Rose? And you, Maisie! What on earth are you doing?'

Rose struggled out, trying not to cry herself. Her head really *hurt*, a horrible sharp throbbing that made her feel sick. Of all the stupid things to do! This was what happened when you started making pictures on baths. Miss Lockwood looked irritable. 'Maisie, you know you're not supposed to take that out of my office,' she snapped, reaching down and seizing the locket. The flimsy chain broke, and Maisie howled even louder, tugging at the trailing end.

Rose could tell that Miss Lockwood was horrified. She really hadn't meant to snap the locket, and she knew how Maisie treasured it. But she couldn't draw back now. 'Silly girl! Now you've broken it. Well, it's just what you deserve.' Red in the face, she stuffed it into the little hanging pocket she wore on her belt, and swept out. 'Go to bed at once! There will be no supper for either of you!' she announced grandly at the door.

'Well, that's no great loss,' Rose muttered, putting an arm round Maisie, who was crying in great heaving gulps.

'She – broke – my – locket!'

'Yes,' Rose admitted gently. 'Yes, she did. But I'm sure we can mend it. Next Sunday. I'll help, Maisie, I promise. And I don't think she meant to. I think she was sorry, Maisie. She could have made us stand in the schoolroom with books on our heads all evening, like she did to Florence last week. No supper's not that bad. It would only be bread and milk.'

'It might not be,' sniffed Maisie, who seemed determined to look on the black side of things. 'It might be cake.'

Rose took her hand as they trailed dismally back to their dormitory. 'Maisie, it's *always* bread and milk! The last time we had cake was for the coronation, nearly three years ago!' Rose sighed. She couldn't help feeling cross with Maisie for getting her into trouble, but not *very* cross. After all, she'd been tempting fate with the windows anyway. Maisie was so tiny and fragile that Rose always felt sorry for her. 'Do you want me to tell you a story?' she asked resignedly, as they changed into their nightclothes.

'Will you make the pictures come again?' Maisie asked, her eyes lighting up.

'I don't know,' Rose told her honestly. 'It's never happened before. And there might be trouble if we get caught, I'm sure it's not allowed.'

'It isn't in the Rules,' Maisie said, pouting. 'I know it isn't.'

Miss Lockwood read the Rules on Sundays before church, so they'd heard them that morning. Rose had to admit that Maisie was right, she didn't remember a rule about making pictures on baths. Which was odd – it must mean that it wasn't a very common thing to do, because the Rules covered *everything*. Even the exact length of an orphan's fingernails.

'It just feels like something that wouldn't be allowed...' Rose said. *Which is why it's such fun*, part of her wanted to add. 'Oh, all right. But I think it needs something shiny for it to work.' She looked round thoughtfully. The dormitory was long and narrow, high up in the attics of the old house. Everything was very clean, but shiny was in short supply. There was hardly room for the girls to move between the narrow, grey-blanketed beds, let alone space for polished furniture.

Maisie followed her, craning her neck to peer into corners. 'My boots are shiny!' she suggested brightly.

Rose was about to say they couldn't be, then realised that Maisie was right. All the girls' shoes were made and mended by the boys from St Bartholomew's orphanage over the wall. They had a cobblers' workshop where the girls had a laundry, so that they could be trained up for a useful trade. Maisie's boots had just come back from being mended, and they were black and shiny, even if they'd been patched so often that there was nothing left of the original boot. If she could make pictures on a bath, why not a boot?

The two girls sat huddled together under Rose's blankets, staring at the polished leather. 'It'll be a lot smaller, if it even works,' Rose warned.

'I don't mind.' Maisie didn't take her eyes off the boot. 'I want to see what happened.'

'It isn't really what happened…' Rose reminded her. 'Just a story I'm making up, you know that, don't you?'

'Yes, yes.' Maisie flapped her hand at Rose irritably, but Rose didn't think she was really listening. 'Show me!'

Long after Maisie had cried herself to sleep that night – heartbroken by the flickering image of her tiny self running through the park and crying for her mother – and the other girls had come chattering to bed, Rose lay awake.

Had she made it all up? It had seemed so real, somehow. *What if I've turned into a fortune-teller?* Rose worried to herself. She didn't *believe* in fortune-tellers. But of course she'd invented it – she'd put in that pink coat, from the little girls she'd seen out of the window. So if it wasn't real, why had it upset Maisie so much? Why had she believed it more than all Rose's other stories? *The pictures*, Rose told herself. *The pictures made it seem too real. I wanted to believe it, too. I'm not doing that again.*

Next to her, Maisie's breath was still catching as she slept, her thin shoulders shuddering, as if she were dreaming it all over again, the lost child that she believed was her, running round the glittering fountain to fetch her boat, then turning back and seeing only other children's parents.

Rose didn't know how she'd done it. This had never happened when she told stories before today. She hadn't done anything differently, not that she could think of. But she must never, ever let it happen again. It was too strong. Rose was sure she'd made it up – or almost sure – but now Maisie had seen it, for her it was real. She would remember it for ever.

Although, Rose thought, as she eventually closed her eyes, *if it were true, the boat would be in Miss Lockwood's office, with the other Relics…* So it couldn't be. It was just a story. But her stories had never frightened her before.

no rainbows.
no pink.
no sparkles.
no ordinary fairytale.

R J ANDERSON

you've met these feisty faeries

6/13 **Knife** **Rebel** **Arrow**

the brand-new

Out
Now

Swift

978 1 408 31263 6 £5.99 Pbk

ORCHARD